7 DAYS

AT THE

HOT CORNER

7 DAYS
AT THE
HOT
CORNER

TERRY TRUEMAN

HarperTempest
An Imprint of HarperCollins *Publishers*

HarperTempest is an imprint of HarperCollins Publishers.

7 Days at the Hot Corner
Copyright © 2007 by Terry Trueman

www.harperteen.com

Library of Congress Cataloging-in-Publication Data
Trueman, Terry.
    7 days at the hot corner / by Terry Trueman.— 1st ed.
        p.   cm.
    Summary: Varsity baseball player Scott Latimer struggles with his own prejudices and those of others when his best friend reveals that he is gay.
    ISBN-10: 0-06-057494-1 (trade bdg.)
    ISBN-13: 978-0-06-057494-9 (trade bdg.)
    ISBN-10: 0-06-057495-X (lib. bdg.)
    ISBN-13: 978-0-06-057495-6 (lib. bdg.)
    [1. Baseball—Fiction. 2. Best friends—Fiction. 3. Friendship—Fiction. 4. Homosexuality—Fiction. 5. Interpersonal relations—Fiction.] I. Title. II. Title: Seven days at the hot corner.
PZ7.T7813Ag 2007   2006003706
[Fic]—dc22   CIP
                                                                AC

Typography by R. Hult
1 2 3 4 5 6 7 8 9 10
❖
First Edition

This one is for Patti

Day 1
(Tuesday)

Third base, defense: Fielding your position at third is tricky—that's why third base is called "the hot corner." You have to be aware that anything can happen at any time. The hot corner is a world of deadly line drives and crazy "bad hops," sacrifice bunts and long, difficult throws; it's a place where a lot of action happens that can make or break your team—and it's all just part of the game!

I love baseball. I mean, I *really* love baseball.

Sorry, let me be more clear: *Baseball* is the most important thing in my life. I'm totally addicted; it's the one thing I've always been able to count on. Hey, I'm not exactly alone: If you Google the word "baseball," you get 135,000,000 hits in .07 of a second—that's one hundred thirty-five *million*. Some people get strung out on meth or heroin, some on porno or Krispy Kremes, some on music, jogging, lifting weights, or on one of the "lesser" sports like hoops or football—but that ain't me. Nope, for me it's baseball above all, baseball or nothing. I'm Scott Latimer, eighteen years old, starting third baseman on Thompson High School's varsity baseball team.

So why is it that when things go wrong, in baseball *and* in life, they sometimes go so hugely wrong? Why can't bad stuff come one thing at a time, so that you can handle that thing, get over it, and just get strong and ready to play a little ball? Why do bad things always seem to happen right when some good thing is out there ready for you to grab? Some great thing that you've worked for and dreamed about, right there, but when you reach for it, all your dreams just die.

It may not be fair to say, but it's my best friend Travis Adams's fault that right now I'm at the Spokane County Public Health building, sitting in an ugly orange vinyl chair. On a small white ticket in my hand is the number 23. What are the odds that when I pulled out a number from the stupid waiting-turn machine, I'd get my uniform number, 23, my "lucky" number? Maybe that's a good sign . . . but I doubt it.

The last number they called was 16, so it looks like I'm going to be here for a while. I've decided to get an AIDS test. I'm not gay; I'm not an IV drug user, either. I'm a third baseman. I shouldn't have to be worried about this stuff, and I know that it's borderline idiotic, or maybe over the borderline, that I'm even here. The chances that I have AIDS are probably low; but still, I need to find out.

This week, of all weeks, I should just be playing baseball. It's almost the end of my senior year—graduation is only a month away—and therefore it's also the end of my high school baseball career. The Spokane All-City High School Tournament starts later today. If we play well enough, and get a little lucky, we'll be in the championship game on Saturday. We've won a record-setting fourteen games in a row, unheard-of at the high school level—so really, this should be a great,

3

amazing time. If I'm ever going to get noticed by a pro scout and get a chance to be drafted by a pro baseball team, it'll happen this week; I've gotta focus on baseball and nothing else—but instead I'm sitting in this uncomfortable chair, waiting to find out whether or not I'm a dead man.

I don't mean to sound melodramatic, but that *is* the situation. I have to be sure that I don't have AIDS so that I can put it out of my mind and just concentrate on playing ball. I can't talk about this with my parents and I won't discuss it with Travis—who doesn't want to talk to me right now either. This is just something I have to do, and something I'd rather do by myself.

I walked in here half an hour ago. It's a stupid-looking building, a nasty brown brick place. When I first came in, I glanced around and found a directory of different programs on the wall. I saw listings for *Unwed Mothers*, *Aid to Dependent Children*, *Substance Abuse*. Great list, huh? Obviously you come here only if you have problems—big ones! And then I spotted it: *HIV Testing—Room 105.*

As I went in the direction of room 105, walking like

4

a condemned man on his way to the electric chair, my mouth felt dry. I could feel my heart pounding inside of me. I hate needles, and all in all this is not a good place to be—I don't want people thinking I'm gay and who the hell wants to find out that you might be sick and never get to play baseball again? As I walked, I also started to feel dizzy. Finally I leaned against the wall for support. My stomach flip-flopped around, sweat broke out on my forehead, and I couldn't seem to catch my breath.

"Are you all right?" I heard a woman's voice behind me.

I looked up to see a middle-aged lady. "Dorothy" said a name tag on her white nurse's uniform. Her expression was kind.

I pulled myself together as well as I could. "I'm fine. I'm just here to have that burger-flipping thing done."

What had I just said?

"Excuse me?" She smiled.

I muttered, "You know, the thing you do to work in restaurants, the health card and the shot thing for handling food." In Spokane, if you want to work in food service, you have to get a shot. I'd planned out the "burger-flipping" excuse to cover my tracks for being in this building in case I ran into anyone I knew.

"Hepatitis B," Dorothy said. "Follow me."

She began to walk toward room 105.

"Isn't that the AIDS room?" I asked, wondering if she knew what she was doing.

She smiled at me again, glancing back over her shoulder. "Blood testing for HIV and hepatitis are done in the same clinic." She slowed her pace so that she could walk next to me.

Hearing that all the blood test stuff is done in the same area made me feel a little more relaxed. If I saw any kids I knew, I'd use my burger excuse, like I'd planned.

So Dorothy led me down here and I've been waiting ever since. In this waiting room, just outside the door marked 105, there are half a dozen other people—thankfully, I don't know any of them. I got the slip of paper marked number 23, and then I also filled out and turned in a little card, putting my number in the upper right-hand corner. When I was sure nobody was watching, I checked the box "Reason for this visit—HIV screening."

That was twenty minutes ago. In that twenty minutes only number 16, and just a minute ago number 17, have been called. When that happens, you walk through the door into room 105 and disappear—no one since I've been here has come back out. Either there's some other exit or they test you, find out you've got AIDS, and just shoot you in the head right there. Just kidding . . . I think.

I look at the other people here, not staring, but noticing them: There's a Hispanic-looking guy, an overweight lady in a floral print big-lady's dress, a skinny guy in his twenties wearing Levi's and a tight black T-shirt—he's the only person who looks sort of gay to me. But the two I keep noticing most are sitting closest to me, a girl about twenty years old and her little kid, about two or three. The girl is kind of cute—but real tired-looking. She looks scared. Her kid is all energy and giggles and climbing all over her, jumping around like a monkey—his mood is the exact opposite of hers.

I'm trying not to stare at them, but it's hard. I keep wondering if she's here for an AIDS test. For herself? For her little kid? These thoughts really creep me out.

In a million years I never would have known or even thought that people sitting waiting for AIDS tests could be so . . . so normal, I guess. I was afraid this place would look like an audition room for *The Birdcage* or some other gay movie, but that's not true at all. Shows you what I know.

Suddenly the mom grabs the little kid and scolds him, telling him to stop bothering people. The little kid looks really mad and his face gets really red, like he's holding his breath. I remember doing that when I was little, holding my breath like that when I got upset. As I look at the other people sitting around, glancing at all their nervous faces, catching glimpses of their scared eyes, I do this thing I've always done ever since I saw a movie once where the grown-ups, still talking like grown-ups, were suddenly little kids, just like they were before they grew up. Looking at the little three-year-old, all red-faced and mad, I imagine these people here in the waiting room with me as they might have been when they were little: Like I can sort of see the Hispanic-looking guy as a little kid; the overweight lady in the floral dress as a skinny little girl, not fat at all; the gay guy in the tight T-shirt, if he even is gay, as a regular-looking little kid with parents and maybe a brother or sister, just doing the kinds of stuff all normal little kids do.

All these people, including myself, were little kids once too, like in that movie I saw, with nothing in the world to worry about. And now, on this particular day, we have all landed in this incredibly scary place—a place you go to sit and wait to get news that will change your life forever, one way or the other. Pretty heavy.

But I still think this test is a good idea for me, a necessary thing to do.

After all, it's been more than six months since Travis Adams's blood was all over my hands, more than six months that the disease could have been brewing in me.

Finally the lady behind the counter calls, "Number twenty-three."

I walk through the door marked 105. After the door closes, latching behind me, another nurse greets me. She walks me down a hallway full of closed doors. About halfway down the hall we stop, and she opens one of them for me to go in.

Sitting there is the same nurse I fed the BS to about "burger flipping" when I first came in. I turn about ten thousand shades of red.

"Oops," I say. It just pops out.

The nurse who led me here asks, "Is there a problem?"

"Not at all, Margaret," the other nurse says, rising from her chair and gently touching my arm. "We spoke in the foyer earlier, but no confidentiality breach occurred." She turns to me. "I'd be happy to be your nurse for whatever kind of procedure you require, if you'd like me to."

"Sure, that'd be great," I say, still embarrassed. I look at her name tag again. "Thanks, Dorothy."

The nurse named Margaret leaves.

"I'm really embarrassed," I say. "I'm sorry I lied."

"There's nothing to be embarrassed about,"

Dorothy says, smiling and looking into my eyes. She motions for me to sit down, and she sits across from me. "You have your own reasons for wanting an HIV screening, and that is nobody's business but yours. Nonetheless, without telling me your name or anyone else's, would you be willing to explain why it is you believe you need this procedure?"

I tell her everything, everything that happened to Travis and me last winter at Spencer's Batting Cages. I tell her all about that day; I've thought about it so much for the last few days that it's like it just happened.

From the street you'd never guess that there could be batting cages in Spencer's. It looks too small; but when you go in, the hallway winds back around, and in the back are three screened-off boxes with pitching machines. Even though there are only a few other batting cages in all of Spokane, there's never a wait for a cage at Spencer's. This is probably because when you're there, you feel like you're in a dungeon. The metal mesh of the cages is old and kind of corroded-looking, like it was once used to trap crabs in Alaska.

The lighting sucks—just bare bulbs. The place is dirty and sweaty and gross. It stinks of machine oil and ten-thousand-year-old Deep Heat ointment. The actual pitching machines look like third world torture devices.

Despite this ugliness I've always *loved* it at Spencer's. This is mainly because first, it's about baseball and anything to do with baseball I love, and second, truthfully, I've never been much with the bat. I'm a good fielder and have a strong arm, which is why I play third, but I've never batted over .350, which sounds hot until you realize that a lot of decent high school hitters bat over .400. It's not that I'm terrible; it's just that hitting is the weakest part of my game. In real games I'm bad at guessing what pitch is coming—heat or junk. I'm going to have to fix this to play pro ball, so I practice hitting a lot, but in batting cages the pitches come slow, moderate, or fast, depending on where you set the dial. So any time you feel like it, you can set the dial where you like it best and *really* hit it! It's such a great feeling: Bang, bang, smack, crack . . .

On a Monday after school, Travis and I went to the

cages. I needed Travis's help there because between pitches he would adjust the dial on the automatic pitcher from slow to medium to fast so that I wouldn't know what was coming, from one pitch to the next. On that particular Monday I'd been hitting for about forty-five minutes and was starting to get tired.

"You want to swat a couple, Trav?" I asked him.

"No," he answered. He always said no.

"Come on, man, we'll set the machine on slow and you can pound a couple outa here," I said.

"Well . . ." Travis hesitated.

This got me juiced, because Travis hardly ever tried to hit and I always felt guilty about having all the fun.

"Yeah!" I hollered. "You da man!" I hurried out of the cage and offered my gray metal Spalding bat to Travis.

"Hold on," I said, and I took off my batting gloves and gave them to him too. They were pretty sweaty but were still better than hitting bare-handed.

Travis held the bat under his arm, like he'd seen me do a million times, and slipped his hands into the blue-

13

and-white gloves, which were several sizes too big for him.

"All right, Trav," I said, handing him my batting helmet, which he forced over his spiky hair. "You *are* da man!"

I walked over to the dial and set it for slow pitches as Travis settled, pretty uncomfortably, into the batter's box. This wasn't the first time he'd ever hit, but he hadn't taken any cuts for quite a while, and it was fun to see him at least trying it again.

The first pitch, traveling about 30 mph, zipped across the plate at knee height, and Travis took the weakest little bailing-out kind of swing you've ever seen.

"It can't hurt you, Travis," I said, instantly wishing I could once in a while keep my know-it-all mouth shut.

"I know," Travis said, getting ready for the next pitch. When it came, he made a much better swing and almost hit it. "You were a little high on that one," I told him. He nodded.

The third pitch he hit square. The sound of the ball on the fat spot of the aluminum bat made that great high-pitched *crack!* sound. Truthfully, I doubt the ball would have carried much past dying-quail territory in left-center field, but I didn't let Travis know that.

"Boom," I hollered. "He got all of that one, folks." I carried on like a mix of great baseball announcers past and present. "And that ball might be, it could be, *holy cow*, it's outa here. Way out on Wave'lin Avenue . . . Get out the rye bread and the mustard, Granny, 'cause it's grand salami time!"

Travis smiled and got set for the next pitch, which he also hit decently. I could tell by his expression that he was having fun.

After a few more good hard hits, Travis started to swing even harder, until finally he took a massive cut at one, missed it, and spun a full 360 degrees, right down onto his butt.

I managed not to laugh, but when Travis looked up, he was already laughing. Then we both noticed that his nose and mouth were covered in blood.

"Geez," he said as the batting gloves turned red, blood dripping from his nose like it was coming out of a faucet. "Sorry," he muttered. I pressed the stop button on the pitching machine and hurried into the cage. Travis, still laughing, said "Sorry" again, holding up my batting gloves for me to see.

"Don't be an idiot," I said. "I don't care about my batting gloves. Are you okay?"

"I got a bloody nose," Travis answered. "How'd that happen?"

"You swung too hard," I said. "I think the bat smacked you in the face when you fell."

"Geez," Travis said, still laughing. "That's impossible, isn't it?"

I said, "Obviously not, since you just did it. No, Trav, anything's possible in baseball—I've seen guys hurt themselves in every imaginable way: I saw a guy drive a tipped foul ball right into his own nuts one time; I saw a guy knock himself out with a ricochet; I saw a guy—"

Travis interrupted me. "Okay," he said, tilting his head back, trying to slow down the blood still dripping from his nose. "I got it, Mr. Baseball. Am I all right?"

"Sorry," I said, and without giving it a thought, I reached across to Travis's mouth and gently lifted up his lip to see how badly he was hurt. I wanted to be sure that all his teeth were still in place. His nose was bleeding from both nostrils, and his upper lip had a tiny cut and was already getting puffy. Blood covered his mouth and chin.

"Are ma teeh okay?" Travis slurred as he tried to talk around my hands.

"Yeah, I think so," I said, still running my fingers across his gum line to make sure that there were no sudden gaps. "You're okay," I reassured him. "You're gonna live."

I felt guilty; like it was my fault he'd hurt himself because I'd pressured him into the cage in the first place. "You're a mess, though," I said.

Travis looked at me. "You too."

I looked down at my hands and there was blood all over them; I held my fingers out, all crinkled, and pointed them at Travis. "I vill drink your blood," I said, trying to sound like Dracula.

He laughed at that one and even more blood dripped from his nose. It took us a while longer to finally stop his bleeding.

· · ·

Dorothy, the nurse, listens quietly as I explain, nodding once in a while, but the look on her face doesn't give anything away about her feelings.

After I've told the story, she nods and smiles and then says, "It's true that HIV is transmitted through direct blood contact—and most frequently that involves an open wound or tear in the flesh or through sharing an unclean hypodermic needle with someone who has the virus—or by an exchange of fluids through sexual contact."

"I'm not gay," I blurt out. It's important to me for her to know that if I have AIDS, I didn't get it because of sex stuff—at least not gay sex.

She says, "Okay."

I add, "And I don't do any drugs at all."

"That's good," Dorothy says. "Has your friend told you that he is HIV positive?"

"No . . ." I say. "It's just . . ." I can't think of how to put it.

"You just want to play it safe?" Dorothy asks.

"Yeah," I say. "I mean, even the trainers on our

baseball team wear rubber gloves when they wrap ankles or wrists, and that isn't even about blood, right? But they're still being careful. Plus I have other reasons to be worried, and my team is on a run at the city championship—it's the most important thing ever. . . . I just can't be distracted by this thing right now. I hope to someday get drafted to play pro ball and . . ." I don't finish this sentence. I feel stupid even saying it, as the chance of my getting a call from the pros is probably slim or none.

Dorothy looks a little confused by my rambling explanation, but at least she doesn't ask me about the "other reasons." Instead she questions me some more about the blood at the batting cages, and I explain about it again.

She asks, "May I examine your hands, please?"

I hold out my hands, sweaty palms up. Wearing white plastic gloves, she turns my hands over and stares at them intently. "You bite your nails a bit, huh?"

My head reels again, and I feel even more dizzy than I did earlier, out in the foyer. The room begins to spin. I drop my head down between my knees to keep from passing out and falling off the chair.

"Whoa!" Dorothy says, putting her hands on my shoulders and steadying me. "You all right?"

I mutter, "No."

Blood to blood! My raw skin where I bite my nails and Travis's blood all over my hands! Sweat runs down from each of my armpits and a sheen of it covers my face. My mind screams: AIDS! AIDS! AIDS! AIDS!

"Breathe deeply now." Dorothy's voice calls to me from somewhere. "Steady, easy, breathe deeply. Come on, you're going to be fine, take it easy."

I follow her directions, and soon the room stops spinning. I sit back up in my chair.

"I'm a dead man," I say.

"Not at all," Dorothy responds. "That's not true at all." She pauses until I look at her.

She says, "Even if your friend is HIV positive, which we have no reason to believe he is, especially given his age and how little we know about his sexual history—even if your friend *is* sexually active, there's no reason to assume that he's infected. You don't get HIV just by being sexual. You *may* get it by having unsafe sex with someone who has the virus."

"*May*?" I ask. "I thought you definitely got it by doing that."

"That's not accurate," Dorothy says, her voice calm and reassuring. "Many people, not knowing that their partners were HIV positive, have had unprotected sex with those infected partners for years without contracting the virus at all. Based on what you've told me about your history, you have a very low risk factor. I wouldn't even recommend an HIV test for you at this time."

"What?" I can't believe she is serious. "What about my fingernails? What about all that blood?"

"I can see how worried you are," Dorothy answers softly. "If you want to have an HIV screening, I'd be glad to do the procedure. If you think it would make you feel better, I'm glad to help."

"Yeah," I answer. "I don't wanna keep worrying about it."

Dorothy smiles again and says, "Okay, roll up your right sleeve."

The procedure is no big deal. Just a regular blood test, I guess. I look in the other direction, not wanting to see the needle go into my arm. Dorothy must have done millions of these, because I don't even feel it. I honestly don't even know she's stuck me until several seconds after she's finished, when she says, "Okay, that's it."

"You're done?" I ask. "I didn't even know you'd started."

She smiles.

Settling back in the chair, I take over the little cotton ball that Dorothy presses against the pinprick. It stings a little, but nothing too bad; now for the scary part. I take a deep breath and ask, "Can you look at it right away? I'd like to get the results before I leave."

Dorothy half smiles and says, "I'm sorry, but it takes five business days to get the results back."

"What!" I hear my voice get loud, almost yelling. I quickly do the math. "Today is Tuesday. If it takes *five* business days, doesn't that mean—Monday! *Monday* before I'll have the results?" I say, still in a loud voice. "Counting the rest of today, Monday is *seven* days away! The tournament will be over by then!"

"I'm sorry," Dorothy says.

I don't say anything. I am stunned.

Dorothy looks at me sympathetically. "I know that these seven days are going to feel like years, but here in Spokane there's just no way for us to do the test any faster. I'm sorry."

I take a couple of deep, slow breaths so that I won't get dizzy again. "Seven days," I say softly to Dorothy.

"Counting today, yes," she says, "but I'm sure the news will be good."

It's the only time I feel that Dorothy has lied to me. Not that she doesn't believe the test will be all right—I don't think that's a lie—but for her to say she's "sure" it will be okay just isn't true. *Not knowing* is why people have to take the test. Only the test can make anybody *sure*.

And the test takes seven days!

Ahhhhh!! All I ever wanted to do was play baseball, and now I'm trapped at a hot corner that's real different than just playing third base.

How did my life change so quickly? Everything was so good, and then blam!

It started two weeks ago.

That's when Travis Adams moved out of his parents' house and in with my dad and me. He wouldn't say exactly what it was his folks were so upset about that he'd had to leave their home. He seemed pretty upset himself. He showed up at our door on a Thursday night at about eight o'clock with a suitcase. He asked Dad if he could stay with us.

"For tonight?" my dad asked, not so much inviting Travis in as getting out of the way; I can't remember the last time Travis rang the doorbell at our house.

"Yeah, for tonight," Travis answered Dad. "Tonight and maybe some more nights too."

"Do your parents know you're here?" Dad asked.

"Yep," Travis said, looking away from Dad, down at the floor.

Dad said, "You're always welcome, Trav."

I know that later the same evening Travis's dad, Roy, phoned my dad and they talked about what was going on, and that Travis's parents said Travis had their permission to stay with us "for the time being." Actually, because he's seventeen years old, Travis can live pretty much anywhere he wants—that's the law in Washington State—but I knew he didn't leave his parents' house on his own, and my dad wouldn't tell me more.

A couple of times since he moved in, I tried to get Travis to talk about what was going on, but he kept saying, "It's kind of private. I'd rather not discuss it."

That was enough to shut me up. But my curiosity had been killing me. I've known Roy and Rita Adams, Travis's parents, for as long as I've known him. They're really nice people. When my parents got divorced I was seven, and I'd just met Travis; his parents became real important to me—the whole family did. I was too young back then to talk much about how I felt about my parents' divorce—in fact, to this day, I've *still* never talked about it with Dad or Mom. What's the point? Yakking about it won't change anything. But the divorce was hard—real hard. I cried a lot. Not many kids in our class had divorced parents, so Travis's friendship and my feeling that I was almost a part of his family was big for me. I'm not saying Trav's parents are perfect; Roy is gone a lot in his work and I've heard

Rita lose her temper and swear more than once, but she's also put her arm around my shoulder and comforted me when I was upset—lots of times, actually. She's always made me feel safe and okay. And Roy is a great dad. He took Travis, Travis's little brother, Hank, who is now ten years old, and me across the state to see the Seattle Mariners every summer for five years: driving us to Safeco Field and back (six hundred miles round-trip), hassling with the traffic, motels, the comic book/baseball card store in the Pike Place Market where we always demanded to go. He put up with all of that garbage just for us.

The first time I met Travis was right after the weekend my dad moved out of our house, a few days after my parents told me they were getting divorced. I was really scared. Travis was new to my school. We were second graders, standing near each other at recess, and out of the blue, like the total wack job I was that day, I just blurted out, "Are your parents married?"

He looked at me kind of funny, but answered, "Yeah."

I said, "Mine are getting divorced."

He said, "Oh," looking at the ground before looking up and adding "Bummer."

I said, "Yeah, I guess."

Then I said, "You know, if one of my parents just died or something, everybody would feel sorry for me."

Travis nodded his agreement, as if what I'd said wasn't pretty nuts.

We were quiet awhile, and then he said, "When they get divorced, though, you'll get twice as many Christmas presents."

I asked, "How do you figure?"

Travis said, "In our church, this girl, Ashley Anderson, her parents are divorced and she said she gets twice as many presents for Christmas and her birthday because her mom and dad feel so guilty or something."

I thought about it a second and said, "Cool." Then I thought more about what I'd said about Mom or Dad dying. "It's not like I wish my parents were dead."

Travis said, "No, yeah, I know what you mean."

I said, "I'm just saying that if one of them died, it'd be easier than a divorce. I hate it."

I started to get some tears in my eyes then, so I looked away from Travis so he wouldn't see.

He said, "You can borrow my parents any time you want. You can pretend they're your parents too, if you wanna."

I asked, "Really?" even though it seemed like a pretty goofy idea.

Travis said, "Sure, I don't care. I've already got one brother anyway—why not have another one?"

We both laughed then. And that was the first time I'd laughed since I'd heard that my own family was blowing apart.

The very next Saturday, Travis and I went together to try out for the first organized baseball I ever played; actually it was T-ball. I was great at it. Trav wasn't. My first time at bat I smacked the ball off the tee and watched the kids in the outfield chase it as I legged it out a triple. From that moment on I was in love with baseball and I've never looked back.

So Travis and his mom and dad have actually been in my life as long as baseball has. Somehow, Roy and Rita kicking Travis out of their house changed everything—I just couldn't get my brain wrapped around it. I couldn't imagine what Travis could have done for such an impossible-seeming thing to have happened—until yesterday, when he handed me a copy of an article that appeared today in our high school newspaper.

Coming Out

by Margo Fancher

A senior in our school is gay. He doesn't want to have sex with every good-looking guy he sees, and he doesn't think of himself as weird, though he knows some of us will think he is. Since "coming out," telling his family he's gay, he's been kicked out of his parents' home. (They don't want him to "influence" his younger brother.)

He's a kid a lot of us know. He doesn't want his name used in this article because he doesn't want to embarrass his family or his friends, but he does want us to know that he's here at our school.

He says that even though coming out to his family has been the hardest thing he's ever done, he doesn't want, or need, our pity. He is not ashamed of who he is. He's gay and he knows other kids who are gay too, though he says he would never "out" anyone else. But he's starting the process for himself; he's coming out.

The reason this student has talked to me is best summed up in this statement from him.

"If I were black and walked into a room, I'd like to think that people would stop telling a racist joke or speaking racial slurs while I was there, but also after I'd walked out. Being gay, I never know what I'll hear when I walk into a room. I can't control what people say after I leave, or even when I'm there, but I can't and won't keep pretending that gay jokes are funny or that homophobia is any more okay than racism."

Our classmate hopes that this article helps increase our sensitivity to his and other gay students' needs. If it doesn't, and where and when it doesn't, he's going to start standing up for himself. He doesn't say this like it's a threat or a warning; rather, he'd like us to treat it as a simple declaration of his right to be treated with the same dignity and respect that every other student here expects and deserves.

It's funny: Not in a billion years would I have guessed the story was about Travis except that he handed it to me himself. In fact, I said, "No way," the second I finished reading.

Here was my best friend for the past eleven years, now living at my house, sharing my food, sleeping in my room, and it just so happens that he's *gay* and I never knew! I stared down at Margo's article for several moments after I'd finished reading. I was afraid to look up at Travis. I knew that when I did look up, I would have to see him differently than I'd ever seen him before, and I wasn't sure I'd still like what I saw.

I asked, "Are you saying your folks threw you out 'cause you're queer?"

Travis said, "Gay. . . . Yeah, they said they didn't want me around my little brother anymore—like he might catch it or something."

"Wow," I said, unable to think of anything else at that moment.

"Yeah," Travis said.

All right, here's the thing: I know that in lots of places, like big cities, the whole gay thing is not that big of a deal. Even here in Spokane the local community college has a club for gays and lesbians and there's a Gay Pride parade every year—but at Thompson High School, at *any* high school in Spokane, for a lot of kids there's still a stigma attached to the whole homosexual thing. I'm just being honest; the word "gay" is even a synonym for "bad," as in "This party is so gay, let's get out of here . . ." or "This pizza tastes gay!" There are "out" gay kids in our school, but they are often kind of ignored, and the best they can do socially, whether anybody wants to admit it or not, is to be left alone. Until this thing with Travis, I never really thought much about what you might call "the gay issue." But then Travis handed me the article.

Truthfully, I felt like screaming at him! I don't need my teammates finding out about Travis being gay and then looking at me, wondering if I'm queer too. Most of them know that he's been my best friend forever and that for the last couple of weeks he's been my *housemate*. Never mind how totally mind-blowing it is to think I know people as well as I thought I knew Trav and his parents, only to find out something like this.

"Gay, huh?" I asked him, unsure of what to even say. "Why didn't you ever tell me before? Why'd you bring this up now, of all times?"

"Margo and I were talking," Travis said. "It just kind of came up, and I didn't feel like lying anymore. . . . Sorry if the timing isn't perfect for you."

He sounded pretty sarcastic with the thing about timing, so I said, "Kind of came up?" not even trying to keep the annoyance out of my voice.

Travis looked at me and said, "I'm not trying to hurt you or your dad or anybody. She was asking about my being out of my parents' house, wanting to write a story for the paper about kids who get kicked out. She asked me what was going on, and I just told her the truth."

I couldn't think of how to ask the next question, but Travis seemed to read my mind. "She's not gonna tell anybody that I'm the guy in the article. She gave her word."

With lots of kids that wouldn't mean squat, but with Margo Fancher Travis's secret is safe. When Margo was only a freshman, she got written up in Spokane's real newspaper, *The Spokane Herald*, for refusing to "divulge her sources" for a school newspaper article she wrote about kids who were stealing cars. It almost went to court, but the cops dropped it when they caught the car thieves and when they realized how serious Margo was about respecting the "confidentiality of the press." Travis is safe from Margo. But what about all the kids who'll try to find out in other ways? And what about me?

"I don't get it, Travis. How could you tell her before you even told me?"

Travis stared into my eyes and answered, "Are you kidding me? Tell you? Yeah, right."

I felt my ears start to burn. "What's that supposed to mean?"

Travis said, "Look how you're reacting."

I heard my voice go up. "I'm reacting fine—what's your problem? I mean, it's cool, you telling her. You did what you had to do, right?" I hoped my words sounded genuine enough, but my heart was definitely not behind them. Really, I wished the whole thing would just disappear.

Although I tried not to let Travis see, I started to feel more and more freaked out. "I can't believe you're gay," I said, looking up at him for about half a second before I looked away. He didn't seem any different, but something was changing between us; at least for me it was. "Are you sure you are?" I asked, staring at the floor and feeling kind of stupid.

"Yeah," Travis said. "Course I'm sure. You think I'd tell you if it was a 'maybe'?"

"I don't know," I said. I felt embarrassed and not in control. "I just . . ." I couldn't think of what I wanted to say or ask. "You can't be gay—it just doesn't fit," I finally mumbled.

Travis said, "I've never tried that hard to hide it, Scott; it doesn't fit for you because you've never looked at me that way, never looked beyond your own life, which mostly revolves around *Baseball Tonight*. It doesn't fit because you're oblivious. "

"That's not true," I said, thinking how completely true it really was; if something is not about baseball, I'm usually not that interested. Still, the whole gay thing, to use a baseball cliché, was definitely coming at

35

me from out of left field.

"Well," Travis said, "whatever. But think about it:
Don't you find it a little bit weird that I've never had a
date with a girl in my whole life, that I've never talked
about getting laid, that I've always changed the subject
every time we even got close to talking about sex?"

I said, "I guess, yeah, but I thought you were
just . . . I don't know . . . shy or something."

Travis said, "Do I seem shy at any other times?"

I answered, "I don't know. . . . No, I guess not."

"I'm not shy, Scott; I'm gay," Travis said.

I asked, "How long have you known this about
yourself?"

Travis said, "Since I was, like, six or seven maybe."

"That's ridiculous," I said. "We never even thought
about sex back then." Even as I spoke, I knew I was
lying. The truth is that when it comes to sex, I've
always thought about it. I fantasized about girls as early
as second grade. So was Travis fantasizing about guys
back then—about *me*, even when we were that little?
Does he fantasize about *me* now?

"I can't speak for straight people," Travis said softly,

36

"but I've always known I was different. It's just the way I am. I tried to pretend it wasn't true, but for as long as I've thought about sex, I've known it."

I thought, So much for truth and honesty between best friends. But I'll admit it: If I had that kind of secret, I'd probably struggle with talking about it too; in fact I'm not sure I'd ever tell anybody!

"Why?" I asked. "I mean, do you know why you're gay?"

"No," Travis said. "It's just the way it is, who I'm attracted to. I couldn't change it even if I wanted to, which I used to want." He paused a moment, then looked at me and spoke clearly. "But not anymore."

We just sat there.

I didn't know what to say to him, didn't know what he wanted or needed from me.

Travis didn't say anything either.

And that was the moment I suddenly remembered the blood all over my hands that day at the batting cages. I tried not to let Travis see my panic, but I'm sure I turned white. I felt a sudden rush of fear, *real* fear, unlike anything I've ever felt before. It was terrible, like getting the wind knocked out of you and almost passing out: My chest ached, my hands quivered.

"What's the matter?" Travis asked. "You look sick."

"I'm fine," I answered, trying to catch my breath.

My stomach felt weak and my skin tingled like a thousand little needles were pressing into me all at once. All I could think about was that day at the batting cages, Travis's blood all over my hands. Could Travis have AIDS? Could he have had AIDS back then? Isn't that a huge risk for gay guys? I knew that not *all* gay people automatically get the disease—I mean, I'm not *that* stupid. But I couldn't stop thinking about it. Travis was gay and I'd had his blood on me.

I just blurted out, "Do you have safe sex? . . . Could I have AIDS?"

Travis looked at me like I'd just kicked him in his stomach. He said, "What do you mean? You and I never had sex."

Just hearing him say it made me sick. "Yeah, of course not, I know we didn't, but what about that day you bled all over me at Spencer's Batting Cages?"

At first Travis looked confused, but then he remembered. "That was way last winter."

I asked, "So I'm safe, then?"

Travis, actually sounding upset, asked, "You think I wouldn't mention something to you if I thought there was any risk?"

"I-I . . ." I stuttered. "I don't know *what* you'd do anymore. I mean, I thought I knew you, but obviously . . ." I could tell by the look on Trav's face that each word I spoke was making things worse, so I didn't even finish my sentence.

But he was already mad. "What kind of friend do you think I am?"

I shot back, "I don't know. I guess a gay one?"

Travis turned red, and said, "If you're worried about AIDS, go get a test. You can get HIV from *any* unsafe sex, you know?"

I knew he was right, and he knew that I'd been with girls before, but *he'd* bled all over *my* hands, and he'd never answered my question about maybe being HIV.

We sat through another awkward silence, and it felt like Travis was reading every negative thought in my mind; he said, "You can't handle this. . . . I didn't think you could."

Stalling, because I didn't know what to say, I muttered, "What?"

Travis said, "You heard me; I knew you'd react this way. My being gay doesn't fit your imaginary view of the world."

"What are you talking about?"

"Look how you are, man—baseball and bullshit—you think everything is the way you wish it were, when really nothing is!"

That *really* got to me. My ears burned even hotter than before; my face and neck felt flushed as I got more and more mad; finally, trying to control my tone, I said, "How am I the bad guy in this thing? You're the one who's gay, who's making some big issue of . . . *coming out*. . . . Big friggin' deal! Why do gay people think all the rest of us need to know that stuff about you? I never get that."

Travis, blushing, snapped back, "You never will, Scott, not as long as you live in fantasyland, a wonderful world where baseball is more important than anything or anybody, where my parents are perfect and your parents are not because they got divorced, where I have to be straight to be all right with you, and . . . man, the list is endless. . . . Fantasyland!"

"Fuck you!" I yelled, surprising myself by how loud I said it. "You never trusted me to handle it before, you never gave me a chance—"

He interrupted, "Well, now's your chance—"

I interrupted right back, "Yeah, *now*, along with every kid in school. Thanks a lot."

He said, "Trust has to be earned."

I felt frozen, unable to say anything more. We just sat there in another long silence. If he said another word, I'd want to beat him up; he probably felt the same way toward me.

But all I could think about were three things: First, every kid in school but especially my teammates finding out about Travis being gay, and all of them thinking that I must be too; second, being distracted when I should be focused on playing ball; and last, about dying, about being *dead* just because I was a friend to Travis Adams. I felt like throwing up. The room swirled around me and I couldn't find the words to tell him how afraid I was. Instead, I looked up and forced a weak smile. I said, "It's cool," although it sounded phony even to me.

Travis didn't smile back and he didn't say another word.

I'd said it was cool, but it wasn't then, and it sure isn't now.

That conversation was yesterday, and we haven't spoke ten words to each other since.

After my AIDS test today, when I get home, the house is quiet. I go straight to my room.

Travis is lying on my bed when I open my door. He's been sleeping on the couch downstairs.

He looks up and asks, "You want the bedroom?"

I answer, "No, I'm good—I just gotta grab my stuff for the game."

He asks, "Where you been?"

I'm not about to admit to him that I was at the Public Health building, getting an HIV test, not after how he acted before, so I say, "Just out, getting gas—nothing much."

We're both quiet.

I'd like to ask him if he's heard about anyone figuring out that he's the guy from the "Coming Out" article—that's what is really on my mind, but I don't know how to ask it without him getting upset again. Thinking this actually makes me kind of mad. So I'm mad that he's mad. Nice, huh? Real mature.

I realize that I've been standing here quiet for a long time, with neither of us saying anything at all. It's weird. I almost feel guilty about not talking. But he hasn't said anything either—why is it my responsibility? Why do I have to be the one to start some ridiculous conversation about things that I don't even want to talk about? Come to think of it, there's *nothing* I could say to him right now that wouldn't take us straight back to my yelling and swearing at him again.

I look at him lying there on my bed, lying on his back, with his arm up over his face, his elbow covering his eyes, like he's trying to take a nap.

I feel a sudden urge to just go over and punch him.

Instead, I gather up my bag, grab my two aluminum bats, and kind of intentionally clank them together so that he can tell I'm moving around and getting ready to leave. He doesn't budge, doesn't move a single muscle. I decide not to say good-bye; I walk to my bedroom door and go out, slamming it pretty hard; hey, it's *my* door!

Third base defense, final thoughts: No matter how well you position yourself in the field, no matter how much you practice and how quick your reflexes, no matter how hard you try, there's no way to anticipate what's coming your way next. It's just the nature of the game; to play is to risk a laser shot or a bad hop or a simple botch job where you take your eye off the ball half a second early. So here's the truth: No matter how good you are, no matter how much you love the game, playing the hot corner can humble you. I'm feeling pretty humble right now.

Day 2

(Wednesday)

Baseball offense: I love the line in the movie Major League *where the announcer says of a player, "He leads the league in most offensive categories, including nose hair. . . ." Of course, in baseball by "offense" what you're talking about is hitting—kind of simple really: "See da ball, hit da ball." But like everything else, it's not that easy. Offense in baseball, if you think about it, actually means risking your life: You have a guy who can throw as hard as anybody you've ever met, standing sixty feet, six inches away. He rockets a hardball, an object with the density of a rock, pretty much at you. We ballplayers call this "fun."*

We won our game yesterday. That makes fifteen in a row. Joe DiMaggio, Shoeless Joe Jackson, Ty Cobb, Babe Ruth, and every other baseball god and legend are smiling down on me right now saying, "Keep it rollin', rookie!"

But I haven't been at school for five minutes this morning when I hear a big uproar behind the gym, near the student parking lot where I've just parked. I'm opening the black storage box on the driver's side of my truck cab when I see three kids running, with another kid following right behind them.

"What's going on?" I ask the kid lagging behind the others, moving as fast as his short legs will carry him.

"There's a fight!" he pants excitedly. "Somebody's beatin' up the gay kid."

Travis! I toss my books in my truck bed and take off running after the others.

When I round the corner, I'm still fifty feet or so from a circle of what looks like a hundred kids. I can't see inside, but the kids watching are silent. It's so quiet that as I run toward the circle, I can hear the sickening sound of a fist smacking into flesh.

I feel a buzz of adrenaline, mixed with a killer dosage of anger and fear. I'm sure that when I get to the middle of the circle, I'll see some big, dumb, vicious Neanderthal beating up Travis.

As I get closer, I hear another punch land and the crowd give a soft gasp.

I see the guy throwing punches: It's Floyd Ingram, a real quiet guy who finally managed to letter in football just this past fall, his senior year. I've never thought of Floyd as being very tough. He's kind of pathetic. He wears his letterman's jacket *every* day, including the very few times I've ever seen him out on a Friday or Saturday night. The only thing he doesn't do in that jacket is shower; by the dirt on the thing, you'd think he'd lettered in 1982 rather than just six months ago. Truthfully, I've always kind of liked Floyd—I've never hung out with him, but he's always seemed like an okay kid. I've always felt sorry for him—until today. I can't see Travis yet, but I hope he isn't hurt too badly. Floyd's face is sweaty and red, and the knuckle above his ring finger on his right fist is bleeding.

"Say you're the fag," Floyd says.

47

"You're the fag!" a voice comes from the ground off to my left. It isn't Travis's voice, but it's familiar. For a second I can't quite place it, but then the kid who has spoken gets up and I see that it's Zeke Willhelm.

I ask the kid next to me, "What's going on?"

"Every time that big guy hits that little guy, the big guy says, 'Say you're the fag,' and the little guy gives him the finger and says, 'You're the fag.' Then the big guy hits him again."

I watch for a few moments and it's just the way the kid described. Zeke isn't punching back. But he keeps bobbing and weaving so that most of Floyd's punches aren't landing very cleanly and they don't seem to be hurting him much. Zeke has an incredibly stubborn look on his face and an attitude that screams, Hit me again, take your best shot, I'll never give up! Floyd sees the finger sticking up in his face and looks pissed. He swings at Zeke, landing a weak grazing shot across the right side of Zeke's face. Zeke barely budges when it hits him.

"Say you're the fag," Floyd says, but his heart isn't in it. He's getting his butt kicked by somebody who isn't even throwing a punch.

"I'm saying it, man. *You're* the fag!" Zeke screams, and pushes his middle finger toward Floyd's face again.

"Okay," I say, stepping into the circle. "That's enough; come on, cool it."

"He's the fag," Floyd says to me, breathing hard, trying to sound tough but obviously sick and tired of the fight.

"I don't really care," I say back. "What difference does it make to you?"

As my question registers, Floyd, surprised, says, "What?" looking at me as though he might punch me, too.

"Take it easy, Floyd. Come on, it's over," I say in a low, nonchallenging voice.

"Hey," Zeke says, staring straight at Floyd, "you're not really a fag." He pauses a moment, then raises his hand, again holding up his middle finger. *"You're not cool enough to be gay!"* he yells.

"Zeke," I snap at him, "knock it off."

For a second it looks like Floyd will punch him again. But instead he grabs at the chance to just walk away, shrugging his shoulders and moving through the crowd as if nothing has happened.

In a matter of seconds all the kids who've been watching just melt away. In less than a minute Zeke and I are standing all alone on the weedy patch of dirt where the fight has just happened. We've been in the same schools together since we were in fifth grade, so I've always known him. When we got to high school, he started doing weird stuff with his hair, making it a different, unnatural color—blue, pink, teal—every few weeks, and he isn't overly fond of bathing. His teeth are sometimes kind of fuzzy, but he's a typical skater kid: I don't think he cares about other people's opinions of him. I've never thought much about him; he's not a baseball player—in fact he's kind of a freak.

"What was that about?" I ask.

"He said I was 'the fag' and wanted me to admit it," Zeke says, suddenly sounding tired and sore. He touches his lip, which is puffy, and the side of his face where it's darkening into shades of reddish blue. "He kept wanting me to say I was the gay guy from the article or to deny it. I wouldn't do either."

"You're not gay," I say. "I've seen you with your girlfriend—you two look like rabbits in heat—why not just say so?"

Zeke looks at me, disappointed. "Come on, Latimer," he says, "think about it. That Floyd guy is an idiot and a bully, gettin' all wigged out over whether somebody's homosexual or not, and he's not the only one. I wouldn't do anything a guy like that ordered me to do—nothing! Much less take the credit for being brave enough to admit something so personal in the school paper." He pauses a moment and looks around at the ground, then spots his skateboard and walks over to it. He stamps down on one end of the board and it flips up into his hands. "Whoever that gay kid is, he's got a lot of guts; he deserves not to have to be afraid of jerks like Floyd. That kid's sexual thing is nobody's business but his own!"

Even though Zeke and I have never been friends—I mean, he's a skate freak and I'm a jock, water and oil—as I watch him walk away, I remember something about him I haven't thought about in years. One time in seventh grade I was at the NorthTown Mall and

Zeke was over in a corner of the parking lot trying to master this trick where he'd jump the skateboard up onto a curb, slide along sideways for a few feet, then jump the board back off the curb without ever dismounting. It looked impossible. I'd finished baseball practice and had gone over to the mall to wait for a ride home from my mom. I sat on the side of one of those raised flower-bed things and watched Zeke for maybe twenty minutes. I was a good two hundred feet away from where he was; he didn't even notice me. He kept trying and trying to do the trick, never making it. He'd slide along and go crashing off. He never fell hard on the cement, but he came close to killing himself almost every time. Looking back, I guess it was really kind of cool. I mean, he was practicing the same way that I practice baseball, just trying to master a skill by repeating it over and over until it becomes automatic. I remember thinking at the time that Zeke was an idiot for trying so hard to do a stupid trick on a stupid skateboard. But now I realize that skateboarding for Zeke is just like playing baseball for me.

And as Zeke walks away, I think about what he just

said about the whole gay thing and I realize that I actually agree with him. What's up with Zeke Willhelm being a better friend to Travis, even if it is incognito, than I am, when they're not even friends?

I'm thinking about the hot corner again, about how hard it can be to play it straight up and right, to know that rocket shots may be coming your way at any instant and that the best you can do is stand your ground, which may not be enough.

Word of the fight is getting around school the way these kinds of stories always do, bigger or smaller than reality but with everybody having an opinion about what happened, especially kids who weren't even there.

Zeke is a total skate-head and already a mild legend of sorts within his group of friends for his amazing skate tricks. But now he has become an instant hero in a lot of kids' minds. Floyd, whose social stock was already a couple of hundred points below zero, hasn't really been hurt by what happened, and in his own mind and that of the gay-bashing population, he probably feels okay too. In reality, looking at the whole thing, "the fight" was pretty much of a draw.

But gossip about Zeke and Floyd's fight has found its way into one of my classes. By third period Mr. Robbinette in World History is ready for us. Zeke's in this class too. The weird fact that something happening in the real world could relate to anything we ever talk about in a class is a miracle—I can't remember a time, other than varsity baseball, when anything real has *ever* happened at school.

We've been studying World War II, talking about Nazi Germany, the rise of the Nazis to power and how their use of propaganda helped them. Today we watch the film *Triumph of the Will*, which shows the way Hitler worked up crowds by screaming and ranting. It's pretty amazing. It's like the German people fell in love with the *way* Hitler seemed so sincere and so dedicated to his beliefs, more than with what he was actually saying. Hitler probably never said, "I think we ought to gather up all the Jews in the world, including defenseless women and children, and gas them to death." He probably never directly said it, but we now know that's what he did. And yet the film shows all these Germans—young; old; good-looking girls; strong, handsome guys—and they all look ecstatic as they listen to that loony up there screaming. I flash for half a second back to the people I saw at the Public Health building waiting to get their AIDS tests—any of those Nazis, if they were alive now, could have been one of us, sitting there in that waiting room. What I mean is that they look like normal people.

After the film, Mr. Robinette starts the discussion. "It wasn't only the Jews that Hitler persecuted and killed. It could be anybody who wasn't an Aryan."

Johnny Little, class clown, interrupts. "Is that anybody not from Arya, Idaho?" He *is* pretty funny some of the time.

Robinette smiles at him and answers. "Something like that. An Aryan, according to Hitler and the Nazis, was a person of pure blood and superior racially to all others. Unless you agreed with the Nazis, went along with their plans and views, you were likely to end up in either a work or a death camp. Jews, political opponents, and anybody perceived to be an enemy was subject to arrest and worse. Although Hitler started out by targeting Jews, it ended up that anybody who didn't agree with him was in trouble. Eventually, Hitler lumped jobless people and the mentally ill and retarded people and gays all together as 'undesirables.'"

Robinette pauses a second and then says, "I know there's been lots of buzz around school recently as a result of the article in the school paper about homosexuality. In Nazi Germany, Jews had to wear a Star of David on their coats so everybody knew they were Jews. At the concentration camps, gays had to wear a pink triangle."

Zeke Willhelm, fat lip and all, still basking in the glory of getting beaten up, says, "If you didn't like somebody, you could just accuse them of being a Jew or gay and the Nazis would take care of them for you, right?"

Mr. Robinette says, "Yes, that happened a lot. But what I hope we can focus on today are the ways, sometimes less obvious and sometimes not, that unequal treatment is still alive. The Nazis' forcing people to wear identification was a blatant, in-your-face example of this, but I'd like you to think about the ways people show their prejudices now—these are perhaps more subtle but are still hurtful. We brand people we're afraid of just as much today as before, not with badges like the Nazis did, but by fear, gossip, and innuendo."

This all makes some sense to me until I glance around the room and make the mistake of looking at Matt Tompkins. Matt plays first base on our team. Teammates are supposed to be friends, and I am friendly with most of the guys, but with Matt it's impossible—for me at least. Matt Tompkins is big, strong, and real quiet. He always has been, even from when we were in the seventh grade. He's been in classes with Travis and me all through our middle school and high school years. He's always gotten by on his bigness and strength and athleticism, but he's a real private guy, and way too serious. Even in baseball he never seems to be having fun. The truth is, I've never liked him and he's never been a friend. We just don't get along.

And right now he's in the back row where he always sits; his jaw is tight and tense, working over-time. He is staring at Robinette. In his expression is a look of horrible concentration, like I've seen on him only in real tough situations on the ball field a few times. Once when we were playing Kettle Falls, they had a guy on third and two outs in a game we led by one run. Both Matt and I, him at first base and me at third, were told to play way up, to prevent a squeeze play (where the batter bunts and the base runner on third charges home). Of course, there's a danger to playing only twenty feet back from home plate. If the batter swings away, which he almost has to do because you're so close that the squeeze play won't work, there's no way you can get a glove up in time to defend yourself. I remember that day, glancing at Matt for just a second, and wondering if he felt as scared as I did. It so happened that the batter took a called third strike, but Matt didn't look afraid, just tense and angry, like he looks right now.

Matt's glare suddenly shifts to me. He stares straight at me and looks sort of crazy. I feel my stomach flip-flop, and I look away from him as quickly as I can. What's going on? Why is Matt Tompkins staring at me?

The final bell, ending the last class of the day, rings and I'm sitting in biology, completely bored—somehow photosynthesis just doesn't cut it with so much else going on.

I'm thinking about the huge pile of negative garbage in my head, when I realize that there is one person I've always been able to turn to when I'm really confused. I've got two hours before our game this afternoon, so I'm going to go visit Travis's mom, Rita. I miss her, and who knows, maybe she'll help me make some sense out of this whole thing.

Maybe I can even talk her into letting Travis move back home (even as I think this thought, I have to admit that I feel a little guilty—some friend huh?).

As soon as school gets out, I hop into my pickup and drive the mile and a half to Rita and Roy's house.

I walk in the door and yell hello, and Rita hollers back "Travis?" from the back of the house—I think the kitchen. It freaks me out, her thinking I'm Travis.

"No," I answer, "it's Scott. Can I come in?"

Actually, I'm already in, and as I finish asking, Rita rounds the corner from the kitchen to the dining room and sees me.

"Hi, Scott," she says, walking right up to me and giving me a big hug. She forces a smile and looks uncomfortable.

I hug her back and smile a phony smile too.

"How are you?" she asks, staring into my eyes, then pulling away from me but still holding my upper arms.

"I'm good," I say.

Rita is a great mom. She always teased and kidded with us, took us to Wild Waters, the water slides over in Coeur d'Alene, during the summer. From when we were little, she always had cookies around, good kinds, too, for snacks.

We walk across the living room, and I sit on the couch while she sits in a little rocking chair right near me.

"Are you all right?" Rita asks.

I feel like saying, How could I be all right? But instead I answer, "Yeah, I'm good . . . kinda stressed."

There is a short, awkward pause; then Rita, ignoring my comment, asks me point-blank, "How's Travis?" Her face looks old and sad now.

Of course, I should have known this question was coming; after all, it's what I came here for, to talk about Travis. But somehow her asking it so directly catches me off guard. It just seems so odd that Rita is asking *me* how her son is. I look into her eyes for a second, but something makes me look away. I don't know; it's like I feel guilty all of a sudden.

"It's all right, Scott," Rita says, reaching over and patting my knee. "It's okay."

"Sure," I say.

Rita takes a deep breath, then speaks in a real soft voice. "We just don't know how to deal with this thing."

I say, "I know, I don't really—"

But Rita interrupts. "We never thought we were prejudiced toward gay people . . . I mean we *aren't* prejudiced—it's just that Travis . . ." She hesitates and I can see tears in her eyes. "He just can't be gay, not my little boy."

I say, "I know. It's so weird, really." Saying this

feels lame to me, and stupid, but nothing else comes to mind.

Rita asks me, "So you and Travis are happy?"

I say, "What?"

She says, "You guys are . . . doing okay?"

It dawns on me that Rita is talking about Travis and me like . . . like we're . . . *together*! I feel my face start to burn.

"I'm not gay, Rita," I blurt out, feeling my whole head turn bright red.

"Of course you're not," Rita says. "Neither is Travis."

"No," I insist. "I mean I'm not gay; Travis and I aren't a couple or whatever you call it . . ." She doesn't seem to be listening to me. I say, "How could you even think that?"

Rita smiles at me. "I care about you no matter what, Scott, you know that," she says softly. But I can tell she doesn't believe me. How can she not know that I'm straight? After all the times I've talked to her about girls, life, my parents, *everything*, how can she doubt me when I'm telling her the truth?

I feel crazy. I want to scream at her, I want to holler, just like I did at Travis, but instead of saying anything, I just sit here, burning up with embarrassment.

Suddenly I understand the real reason I've come here—it was to somehow get back that feeling of the way things had been before Roy asked my dad if Trav could live with us. I wanted to just walk in, raid the fridge, and BS with Rita. I wanted her to be my second mom again, to be here for me and talk to me and tell me that everything was gonna be all right. I wanted Rita to reassure me in ways that my real mom and dad couldn't. After all, my parents split our family apart for reasons I still don't understand. I wanted to know that, somehow, everything was the same between Rita and me. But the opposite of what I wanted has happened: My fears about losing Rita and Roy were right on—they're not here for me anymore; maybe they never really were. I remember what Travis had said to me: *You think my parents are perfect. . . .*

Now that Rita thinks Travis and I are some kind of gay twosome, everything has changed. Roy and Rita live in this nice, pretty house and she bakes cookies and he goes off to work, but when their son really needs them, they're not here for him. And they're definitely not here for me either.

Sitting in the Adamses' living room, I look at Rita and feel—I don't know exactly how to describe it . . . still embarrassed about her thinking I'm gay, but mostly . . . I hate to say this, but mostly I feel ashamed of her for what she's doing to Trav.

Nothing she's said helps any of it make any more sense. I feel depressed. I'm so disappointed in her, and maybe in myself. Mainly, though, I feel awful for Travis. Nobody in his family is on his side.

I get up from the couch.

"I gotta go, Rita," I say.

"Of course, Scott," she says with another fake smile. We walk in silence to the door, where she gives me another awkward hug.

She looks me in the eyes as we finish hugging. "Tell Travis that we . . ." She pauses, and the tears I saw a few minutes ago come back. "Tell him that I'm sorry, but with his little brother here, until he can figure out how to be . . . until you guys realize . . ." She pauses again and finally just says, "No, forget that; just tell him we miss him and that I'm sorry."

I nod my head numbly. "Sure, Rita," I say, trying not to show how sick I feel. I just want to get out of here. My chest hurts and my palms are wet.

I make it out the door. I jump down off the porch onto a little path leading toward the driveway. This path is a line of heart-shaped cement bricks, set down low in the grass. In all the times I've been to this house, I've never paid any attention to these stupid little heart-shaped stepping-stones before. But I notice them now; cement hearts: Yeah, that's about right.

You live in fantasyland . . . where my parents are perfect and yours are not because they got divorced.

"Up yours, Travis," I whisper to myself, but I realize that I don't really mean it anymore.

After talking to Rita, I feel terrible, even worse than before. Thank god I've got a game in an hour. Thank god for baseball.

Baseball offense, final thoughts: You step up to the plate and tap the dirt out of your cleats. If you're successful one time out of every three, you'll end up in the Hall of Fame, so even if you're really good, your chances of failing are pretty high. A good hitter has to stay calm and centered, keep his weight balanced and his emotions under control, and if he does all that and does everything else just right, he'll still probably not get a hit. Makes you wonder, doesn't it? Why even play?

Day 3

(Thursday)

Keeping your head in the game: Whether on defense or offense, you have to keep your head in the game, and to me this means that you have to know what's going on in every situation and how things change with everything that happens. This means that a man on second with two outs is a whole different concern than a man on first with one out. Keeping your head in the game just means knowing what is going on!

What *is* going on?

Well, first off, we won again yesterday. It was great. In baseball the worst teams *win* a third of their games and the best teams *lose* a third of theirs—so how can

67

our team win *16 games in a row*, like we've done this season? Such things are extremely rare, almost impossible; believe me, I've subscribed to *Baseball Weekly* since I was nine years old, and there are winning streaks, but an undefeated season like we're having is unheard of. Okay, for a little perspective: The most wins in a row in Spokane high school baseball history, before our team this year, was 13, back in 1954! *1954!* Wasn't Teddy Roosevelt president then or something? And get this, that 1954 team was from Gonzaga Prep, and they didn't even go undefeated that season—they lost in the semifinals of the city play-offs.

So the answer to the question "What is going on?" is that *we are*—Thompson's baseball team!!

Still, I have to admit it, the rest of life at school is happening too. But it's been three days since the "Coming Out" article hit the newsstands at Thompson H.S. Three days since my HIV test. So far as I can tell, nobody has ID'd Travis, nor has he gone any more public. Truthfully, the excitement caused by the article has quieted down a little bit. Although the question of Who's the gay guy? is still a semi-hot topic in the cafeteria and hallways, mostly it's not angry, more like just curious.

Actually, more and more students have started to notice what we're doing in baseball—we got a big write-up in this morning's *Spokane Herald*. The article even mentioned me and two other seniors by name. It was pretty cool. We're getting a little bit famous. Of course, that also means more pressure.

It's just before our game today. I've been hoping that the whole gay thing has maybe died away completely, but as we're changing, getting suited up, Willie Brown, our second baseman, and Tom Archer, our left fielder, joke about the article.

"It's not one of you guys, is it?" Matt Tompkins asks, gruff and serious.

"Not me," Tom says, laughing, "but I think Willie might be yer man."

"That true?" Matt asks, turning toward Willie and squaring up.

"*No way!*" Willie says. He's a full head shorter and probably twenty-five or thirty pounds lighter than

Matt. "I'm no fag!"

"Hey." Josh Williams's voice comes from the other side of the bank of lockers. He steps around and stands looking at all of us. "*Fag* is derogatory slang," he says. "It's offensive."

"Sorry," Willie says.

Josh plays center field on our team and is also team captain. He's a senior and a three-year letterman in football, basketball, and baseball, a pretty fantastic athlete. He's also an excellent student. Josh is popular in the sense of being widely known in our school. How many really close friends he has I don't know. I never see him out much. Travis and I always call him Josh Flanders behind his back, after the Flanders family on *The Simpsons*. Led by the dad, Ned, they're the perfect "All-American" family, the opposite of the Simpsons. For the Flanders family, who are always happy and successful, "darn" is a swear word. That's Josh Williams—scary, squeaky clean. If it's possible to be *too* good . . . Josh is that. I often feel a little less than fresh when Josh is around, and when it comes to moral certainty and self-assurance, nobody is about to step up against Captain Josh.

I feel a tiny rush of appreciation for Josh's speaking out against antigay stuff until he speaks again.

"The fact is," Josh adds, his voice cool and certain, "homosexuality is a sin against God and nature. We should feel pity for gays and try to help them get better whenever we can. I feel sorry for that kid in the article, whoever he is."

Everybody is quiet. I want to say something, but what words would I use? If I speak up, what will everyone think of me? I know I don't agree with him. If my dad were here, he'd make Josh look and sound like an idiot. But I'm not my dad.

Before I have a chance to say anything, Matt speaks up again. He says to Josh, "Whatever you say. But don't let me catch any of you guys playing fag . . ." He interrupts himself and grudgingly corrects, "Playing gay crap with each other around here. Whatever anybody does in private is their own business, but keep it private or you'll have to deal with me."

He sounds mad—not too surprising, since he's *always* sounded at least a little bit mad the few times he's ever said anything. The thought of Matt discovering that Travis is the "secret gay" from the "Coming Out" article is scary to me—even though Matt says that if the gay kid keeps it to himself he'll be all right, I don't trust that for a minute. Somebody like Matt could hurt Travis pretty badly if he wanted to.

My comfort level isn't exactly increased by the feeling I have that once again, just like in World History yesterday, Matt seems to be addressing himself more to me than to the others. It's almost as if he keeps trying to look at the other guys, especially Josh, but he can't stop from looking right at me. What? Does he think *I'm* the guy in the article? I try not to blink or break eye contact with him, but I can't hold on; I look away. Am I just being paranoid?

My ears are still burning, my head is reeling; as I lace up my spikes and run out onto the field, I wonder if I'm going nuts.

I play one of the worst games of my life, striking out *four* times on mediocre breaking balls. In baseball this is called getting the "golden sombrero," and it's a bad thing, a *real* bad thing for a guy who fantasizes about someday being good enough to actually make the pros. Unlike pro football and pro basketball, where high school guys usually go to play their sports in college first, most good baseball players start their careers right after high school—that's why baseball players are called "the boys of summer."

Right now, though, I'm playing more like "the boy in the toilet"! In our first three games of the tournament my batting average is .233 (3 for 13), more than a hundred points below my regular season average and about one measly base hit above the Mendosa line, a numerical zone below which baseball players disappear like dinosaurs in a tar pit. I'm not able to hit anything that doesn't come straight over the plate, fast. Pitchers are not stupid. They just keep throwing me off-speed junk, curves and sliders and changeups. When I do get a fastball, I'm so completely screwed up that I might as well be swinging one of those little twelve-inch toy bats they sell as kiddie souvenirs.

I know that the stuff going on in my life outside of baseball is having an effect on my play. At least, that's the excuse I'm making for myself, but it's gotta be partly true. For instance, Travis and my dad sat up in the bleachers yesterday and again today, watching me play. They looked ridiculous—a real Hallmark-Kodak moment. I kind of hated them for it—nice, huh, being mad at Dad and Trav for being there to support me?

I'm not as good a person as my dad is. Lots of kids I know talk like they hate their parents, but to be honest, my dad is pretty cool. He and my mom have always shared custody of me, although I spend more time with him, Monday through Thursday. This is partly because he lives in town, where school and all my friends are, and partly, to be honest, 'cause he's less strict than Mom.

But seeing Travis sitting there with Dad in the stands today reminded me of what Matt was saying about the secret gay kid. The thing about Matt that's always bugged me is that, though he's usually quiet, when he does say something, it never feels quite right to me, never feels like he's saying what he really means; I can't explain it better than that, but I don't trust Matt.

In the locker room I grab all my gear as quick as I

can. I want to get home and warn Travis about what Matt was saying before the game today.

I pull into the driveway and go into the house. I go up to my room, where Travis is sitting at my desk studying.

"Travis," I say.

"Yeah?" he says, sounding a little pissy but turning toward me.

I ask, "Aren't you worried about kids putting the whole 'unknown gay' thing together with you being kicked out of your parents'?" I know I sound like a jerk, but I don't have the patience for politeness.

"I don't really care," Travis says. "You're the one who's worried about that."

"Well, yeah, maybe I don't care and for selfish reasons." Then I say, "Sorry," a little bit sarcastically—hey, it's not just *me* who's been avoiding *him*.

"Come off it," Travis snaps, staring straight into my eyes. "You haven't talked to me for how many days now? Is this your idea of being a friend?"

I look right back and say, "Hey, pal, that's a two-way street. You said some pretty mean stuff to me, you know. I'm sorry I've been kind of a jerk, I feel bad, but I've—"

But Travis cuts me off. "Yeah," he says. "That's a little problem you have, isn't it? *I . . . I . . . I.*" Then he turns his back.

Now I'm totally steamed again. "*Me?* What about *you?* Don't you think you're being selfish? This gay thing affects all of us—your friends, your family; I even went and talked to your mom about it."

Travis turns back to me; his expression looks horrible, like I just kicked him in the 'nads. "You did what?"

Suddenly I feel really uncomfortable, ashamed or guilty or both. "That wasn't okay to do? I mean . . . I wasn't trying to . . . I just—"

Travis interrupts, tears in his eyes. "What did she say?"

I look away from him. I feel sad, and *really* bad for him. "She said to say hi," I answer, like an idiot. I glance up real quick to check what Travis looks like; his eyes are even wetter . . . I feel *terrible*.

I say, "She said to tell you she loves you."

Actually, Rita never said this—but I say it to Travis anyway because it's what she *should* have said. I may be mad at him, but I can't help but feel awful that he's so miserable.

Travis looks away and tries to nonchalantly wipe his eyes. He says, "Oh, yeah?"

I say, "Yeah, for sure."

Travis takes a couple of slow, deep breaths and then stares back down at his book and says, "I gotta do this trig."

I say, "Okay," glad to have an excuse to get out of here. I'm sorry about talking to your mom."

Travis doesn't say anything, just pretends that he's studying again.

I quietly leave the room, realizing that I never even told him about Matt Tompkins—but that will have to wait; I'm not going back in there right now.

I go downstairs and walk into the kitchen. Dad has gotten home, and when he sees me he asks, "You doing okay?"

I say, "Not really," and then, speaking softly, I add,

"I wish Travis would move out."

"Why?" Dad asks.

I tell Dad why Travis has been living with us for the past couple of weeks. Dad listens and nods and says, "Yeah, both Travis and his dad talked to me about this already."

"Well?" I ask.

"Well what?" Dad asks.

"Don't you think it's kind of weird, all this stuff?"

"I don't know, Scotty," Dad says. "Not really. It's just life."

"Dad!"

"Scott," he says quietly, "Travis is your friend and I don't care what his sexual preference is—that's his business, not yours or mine or anyone else's. Besides, it's not really about 'preference' anyway—nobody chooses who they're attracted to, so 'preference' isn't the right word—it's just about who Travis is."

I say, "Roy and Rita obviously don't feel that way about it."

Dad says softly, "I know." Then he looks away from me and says even softer, "And that's a shame."

I swear this whole gay thing doesn't amount to a pimple on the butt of the universe to my dad.

We're quiet for a few seconds, then finally I admit, "I'm tired of this gay stuff, I guess. Every time I turn around, I'm scared that somebody will think I'm queer too. I'm sick of it."

"*You're* sick of it!" Dad exclaims, unable to keep the annoyance out of his tone. "How can *you* be sick of it? Travis is the one who's paying the dues on that deal. His parents won't let him in their home. He hasn't asked you for anything, and as near as I can tell, you've been really accommodating in giving him exactly that . . . nothing."

"I can't help it," I say, feeling madder each second. "I'm not as *nice* as you are! I don't even know what I could do to help. I'm really messed up; I don't get any of this!" All of a sudden I feel like I might start punching walls and breaking things.

Dad seems to see this and he backs off. "It's been a tough thing for both of you, Scott. I know that, but there's nothing to get." His voice is softer and real understanding. "Travis is gay, but he's still your friend."

I say, "I know that, but . . ." I can't even find the words for what I feel.

Dad asks, "What else is going on?"

I tell him about the fight at school, how scared I was that it was Travis getting beaten up; I tell him about what Matt said about "the gay guy"; and I explain a little about the arguments Travis and I are having and how bad that feels. I almost tell him about the batting cage and blood and all that, but I hold back—if the news there is bad, there'll be time later for us to discuss it.

I say, "I'm not like you, Dad. I just can't be calm about this."

He smiles and says, "You're a good person, son, a great person. And this is all part of growing up, as clichéd and simplistic as that sounds—it really is." Then he adds, his voice gentle, "But a lot of this stuff really has nothing to do with Travis being gay—you know that, right?"

I say, "I don't know *anything* right now, except that I feel really screwed up."

Dad and I have always been close, always been honest with each other—and I know that he'd never do what Travis's parents are doing, *never*, no matter what I did!

Dad puts his hand up to his chin and strokes his beard gently. I see the wrinkles around his eyes; I notice how old his hands look and the white hairs in his beard and at his temples. Dad's always seemed big and strong to me; he still does, even though I'm now taller than him.

He takes a slow, deep breath, and then says, "Trav doesn't have anyplace else to go right now." His tone is soft and reasonable. "He needs us to be his friends, Scott."

I say, "Yeah, I know that. I don't even really want him to leave, but I don't know how to handle this. It's like he's a different person now. I know he isn't, but that's how it feels."

I look away from Dad and try to focus on something else. On the radio the Mariners are playing, but they're no help, trailing 11 to 2 in the seventh. It feels like *everything* sucks right now.

Dad says, "Maybe you should spend the next couple of days out at your mom's, give both you and

Trav a little breathing room."

I can tell that Dad isn't saying this like a threat, or because he is mad at me. He just wants me to know that if I want to go to my mom's house to stay tonight, on a day that I usually spend with him, it won't hurt his feelings. Dad has to have noticed the tension here too, both Travis and me tiptoeing around each other, avoiding eating dinner together, doing everything we can to keep our distance.

I think about Dad's suggestion to go to Mom's place, realizing that I haven't even spoken to her since all this stuff started. "Yeah," I say, "that'd be good."

Dad says, "I want a hug."

It's ridiculous, you know, a guy still liking a hug from his dad at my age—but ridiculous or not, it feels good.

I feel better, not all the way better, but better. I finish a Raspberry Twister, then go upstairs and take a quick shower. I come back downstairs, ready to head to Mom's place.

The M's have lost, but somehow I don't care. After saying good-bye to Dad, I take off.

• • •

There's a Safeway right around the corner from my house, and I decide to run in and grab a snack for the drive out to Mom's. It's not that far, but I kind of need a junk food rush.

I drive a yellow 1989 Toyota 4x4 pickup truck. I know that 1989 sounds really old, but I love my rig. It's a short-bed SR5 with big oversize tires for off-road driving (which I never actually do). I keep it in pretty nice shape: great chrome wheels, a decent sound system, sheepskin seat covers, and a heavy-duty storage box bolted onto the pickup bed, just behind the cab. Yeah, I love my truck; I even tried to get my dad and mom, separately or together, to go in on personalized license plates for me. I checked with the department of licensing and both "Hotcorner" and "Baseball23" (my uniform number) were still available, but my parents said no. I guess that really would have been sort of show-offy.

But because my truck is bright yellow, I think a lot of kids know it's mine, and as I pull up and park, I see a couple of ninth-grade girls I recognize from school watch me get out and walk into the store.

I'm standing at the chips rack, trying to decide between Cheetos and Doritos, when the two girls approach me. I don't even notice them until they're right next to me. They're only frosh and real young-looking.

The taller of the two, a blond girl, asks, "Aren't you on Thompson's team?"

I say, "Yeah, the baseball team."

The other girl says, "Like there're any others. . . ."

I smile and say, "Don't let the tennis, golf, or track-and-field guys hear you say that."

They both laugh, and the blonde says, "We read about you in the paper this morning."

I say, "Oh yeah?"

"Yeah," they both answer at once.

The shorter girl says, "You guys are awesome; you play third base, huh?"

I smile again. "Yeah, I do. Have you guys been coming out to our games?" Kind of a stupid question, but I can't really think of anything else to say.

"Yeah," they both say again, nodding their heads at the same time.

They look so incredibly young to me, more like sixth graders than high school girls. But they're cute, and someday they'll be the kind of girls who would refuse to even glance at me at a dance or something. Right now, though, they look all starry-eyed and happy.

I make my junk food decision and reach for the Doritos, a medium-size bag, when the blonde suddenly asks, "Can we have your autograph?"

I look at them closely to be sure they're not kidding. Nobody has ever asked me for an autograph before, and it seems ridiculous, but they look sincere.

I say, "Come on, why would you want my autograph? I mean, we go to the same school, right?"

The shorter girl speaks right up. "You're gonna be famous someday."

I laugh and say, "Not too likely."

The blonde says, "You're already famous! Your name is in the paper today."

I say, "Yeah, it's in the box scores every day too, but—"

"No," the blonde interrupts, "it was in the article about Thompson. You're Scott Latimer, and it said you're one of the best players on the team."

I feel myself blush. "We've got a lot of good players—I'm just one of the guys."

The short girl says, "You're a senior."

I say, "Yeah."

"Next year you'll be a big league player—you'll get like five million dollars a year or something."

I keep myself from laughing and say, "The stars get that. Not regular players—"

The short girl interrupts me. "No," she says. "The stars, like A-Rod of the Yankees, get twenty-five million dollars a year—but some pitchers, even guys with ERA's over five, still make millions."

I laugh, surprised that she's so smart about baseball. I say, "That's true, but anyway, there's no guarantee that I'll even make the pros."

"You will," the blond girl says. She asks again, "Will you give us your autograph, please?"

Seeing that they're serious and feeling my face turn redder than the Doritos package in my hand I say, "Sure, I guess."

They both smile and clap their hands. The shorter girl pulls out a Sharpie and two pieces of paper from the back pocket of her jeans, like she had this autograph thing all planned out ahead of time.

She asks, "Will you make them to Angela and Davita?"

I say, "Sure," taking one more glance at them to be certain this isn't some kind of practical joke. I look around to make sure some joker isn't watching and laughing at the end of the aisle. But the coast looks clear, and the girls seem to be completely into it. I have to ask how to spell "Davita" and then I sign my first-ever autographs.

"Thanks," they both say at the same time.

I say, "Sure."

The shorter girl, Angela, says, "Good luck with the rest of the tournament—I know you guys are gonna win it."

Her friend says, "Yeah."

I say, "I hope so, thanks."

"Thank you!" the blond girl says, and stares into my eyes. I glance back, and suddenly she says, "You're cute."

The short girl kind of screams, "Davita, you promised!"

Davita quickly says to her friend, "I'm sorry." Then, turning to me, she says, "But you are."

I blush even worse and look down at my Doritos. I say, "Thanks. . . . It's nice meeting you both. See you out at the games."

Angela grabs Davita and begins to pull her away, saying, "Yeah, we'll see you there. Forgive Davita, she's brain damaged, one too many foul balls off her skull."

"Shut up!" Davita says to Angela, then looks back at me, staring into my eyes again. "See you."

I just smile at them.

Back in my truck driving to Mom's, for the first mile I feel really happy and full of myself.

I'm famous.

I'm gonna be a great baseball player.

I'll make the pros and be rich and happy and . . .

I just miss the green at a stoplight on the corner of Seventeenth and Grand. It's a busy intersection with signals from all directions: east, west, north, and south; and four different left-turn lanes with lights of their own. I'm on Grand, facing south, when all of a sudden, out of nowhere, a cat races into the middle of all this traffic.

I guess you'd call it an orange tabby: orange striped with flecks of white mixed in with the orange. It runs right in front of my truck, with cars streaming by from both my left and right, and now it just stops in the middle of the street and looks right up at me.

Cats' eyes are so strange-looking. Cats stare at you completely differently than dogs do: Dogs always look like they want to know you, but when a cat stares, it's like it's daring you to look back at it; it's just a weird feeling. Does this cat know how much danger it's in? A cat with eight of its nine lives left wouldn't stand a chance in this traffic—but this one isn't moving, it's just sitting out between the two lanes, staring straight at me as cars and trucks and SUVs and vans drive by it.

I freeze. If I honk my horn, it might run into the path of a car and get killed; if I jump out and try to stop the traffic or grab the cat, it might get scared and run anyway. The only thing keeping it alive this second is that it's just sitting still; but how long until a car drives too close to the middle line and runs it over? None of the other drivers seem to even see it. I don't know what to do! Just when I don't think I can stand it for another second, the cat shoots off across the street, heading away from me. Two cars drive right toward it, but by some miracle, some totally perfect bit of luck, they miss it. The last I see of the cat, it's running through a gas station parking lot, leaping up, and clawing its way over a wooden fence into the backyard of a small house.

The car behind me honks—not just a little *beep-beep*, either, but a long blast. I look up and see that my light has turned green, so I ease forward.

I drive on thinking about the cat, about Travis, about my inability to make things okay. Before I realize what's happening, my whole feeling of happiness from the girls at the Safeway has completely collapsed. Famous? A pro? A millionaire jock? Come on! I can't even handle my own life: My parents got divorced; I don't know what to say to Travis; I can't save a suicidal cat; I struck out four times today.

Baseball legend?

Big-shot sports hero?

No way!

The whole rest of the drive out to Mom's, I feel worse and worse, absolutely stupid and worthless.

Mom's house at Weaver Lake used to be Mom and Dad's place before I was even born. We all three lived there together until I was four and they split up. For several years after the separation Dad would stay overnight sometimes and they "tried to work things out," until they finally gave up for good and got the divorce. And that divorce changed everything forever—at least for me it did.

Although the town is also called Weaver Lake, Mom's house is right on the lake itself, twelve miles southwest of Spokane. I pull my truck into my parking spot next to the fence and look out at the wind gently playing across the water. Against my will I say to myself that Weaver Lake would be as good a place as any to lie around and die of AIDS. I gotta knock this off; I don't even know if Travis has ever had sex with anybody before, much less whether he's infected. I've been acting totally stupid.

I open the truck door and climb out. I love the smell of the lake: kind of a seaweed-meets-fresh-air scent. Off the shore from our house, about a hundred yards out, there are some big rocks. Seagulls and ducks hang out there. Twice a year Canadian honkers, a huge gaggle, show up and hang around for a couple of weeks. Mom and I have always taken walks along the lake, and it's beautiful. For a guy my age, the line between boring and relaxing can be pretty thin sometimes. But at Mom's, even though there's really not much to do, it's almost always good; I guess you'd have to call it peaceful.

When my dad lived here, he built a space in the back of the garage that he called a studio. He put up a wall and insulated it and rewired it for lights and an outlet. He even put in a baseboard heater. I walk into the studio now, clicking on the light. I called Mom from

Dad's house to ask if I could come out, and she was really happy that I'd be coming, but I want a few minutes to myself before I see her. A few years ago I turned the studio into my space, a place for my friends and me. Now, when I come out to stay with my mom, I always spend at least one night up here, away from the main house. It's kind of like having my own little apartment. Over the years Travis and I have spent a lot of nights here. I sleep in the little loft and Travis sleeps on the foldout couch. We've had some great times: eating junk food, talking until all hours of the night, watching ball games on my little black-and-white TV with its weak signal for channels 2 or 6 from Spokane, the only stations we could get. Those times all feel like ancient history now. I miss them. I miss him.

I stand in the studio looking out the window, down toward the lake. I start thinking about everything: the baseball championships, Travis, his folks, AIDS, and then about my mom and dad. What did Travis say? *You think your parents are not okay because they got a divorce. . . .*

I think about how sad I was back then. I can see

the old sandbox where I played as a little kid, the boards all weathered and splintery now from so many years exposed to the winds from the lake. I remember how young my mom looked back when we built the sandbox, how big and strong and invincible my dad seemed. I remember him lifting me up and flying me around the yard like I was Superman. I swear I can almost see the outline of his footsteps in the grass.

I look out past the huge old pines in our yard, down to where the waves wash silently onto our beach. And suddenly I start crying. Not just a little teary-eyed boo-hoo, but the real thing. I'm sobbing so hard that it hurts my chest and ribs and drives me to the floor. I can hardly catch a breath. I lie here in the studio all alone on the floor and I cry and cry. I'm ashamed and totally embarrassed. But the weirdest part about this crying is how good it feels, so good and so terrible. I lie here and I think about all those at-bats when I couldn't hit the ball to save my soul; I think about not being able to talk with Trav and not really being there for him when he needs me. I think about when I was a little kid wondering why my parents stopped loving each other.

My crying is so heavy that my body aches. I wrap my arms around myself to keep from flying apart. I can't breathe. I feel like I'm drowning.

After a while I finally get control of myself. It feels like something has lifted off me, like kicking off a heavy blanket when you're mostly asleep but way too hot. My head hurts a little and my body still feels sore—actually, "trashed" is more accurate—but somehow I feel better. In fact, I feel the best I've felt in days. Actually, I feel a tiny sense of peace. I don't know why, but I just do.

When I'm recovered enough so that maybe Mom won't be able to tell I've been crying, I walk down to the house from the studio.

We have two dogs, Evander and Bob, who charge up the yard to meet me. Despite the common wisdom on the subject, having dogs has never done anything much to help me grow up. The truth is, Mom always done more of the work of taking care of them than I have. She feeds them all the time I'm at Dad's and most of the rest of the time too. She cleans up the dog crap because, honest to god, it makes me gag to do it. Despite my complete worthlessness when it comes to doing my fair share with the dogs, I really love them. It's embarrassing how much I baby them, and how I talk to them, calling them moronic nicknames like Baby Bobbie and Pretty Girl. If Matt Tompkins heard me with the dogs, he'd be sure he'd found the girly-boy.

The dogs love me too. We go for walks together every week. I only leash them up when it's absolutely necessary, so they get to run free through the woods on the west side of the lake and over the wheat fields to the south. Right now, I wish I were just a dog, running along all happy and stupid and totally unworried, crashing through the brush and over the pine needles and splashing through the shallows of the lake, freaking out the ducks. *You live in fantasyland* . . . Yeah, maybe, but right now I'm stuck being a human, so I walk into the house.

"Hi, sweetie," Mom says, turning toward me and smiling.

"Hi," I answer.

"Are you hungry? Can I fix you something to eat?" My mom is exactly the kind of person who, up to her elbows in dishwater, asks me if I'd like to dirty some more dishes.

"No, I'm good," I say.

"It's such a treat to have you here on a Thursday night," Mom says. "I can't think of the last time you were out here on a Thursday—"

She stops right in the middle of her sentence the second she looks closely at my face for the first time since I came into the room.

"What's wrong, Scotty?" she asks, staring into my eyes.

I try to smile at her. I walk across the kitchen and plop down onto the big overstuffed couch that runs along one wall of the kitchen–dining room area. From here I can talk to Mom and look out the windows at the lake.

Where do I even start? With Mom, actually, anyplace will do. I ask, "Have you heard about this stuff with Travis?"

Mom says, "Yes, your father told me."

I ask, "Well?"

Mom says, "Well, what? I'm sorry, I don't know what you're asking me."

I ask, "Do you think I live in a fantasyland all the time?"

Mom says, "Actually, that thought has never occurred to me. Do you?"

I say, "Travis said so."

Mom asks, "But he said that when you two were quarreling, right?"

"Yeah," I answer. "Right before I screamed 'fuck you' into his face!"

"Scotty!" Mom's not a big fan of what she calls "the F word."

"Sorry," I say. "Yeah, we were arguing—he was for sure mad at me."

Mom asks, "What else did he say?"

My palms are sweaty and I feel my heart pounding hard, but I decide to just spit it out. "He said that I treat you and Dad like you're not great parents because you got divorced—he said it like anybody who knew me would think that I felt that way, and that it's fuck—sorry . . . that it's messed-up that I think that."

Mom asks, "Do you feel that way?"

I answer right away. "No, not at all—I don't know why he'd think that or why he'd say it."

Mom says, "You two were arguing; people say lots of things when they're angry."

I say, "Yeah, and I was being pretty hard on him about the whole 'gay' thing—I couldn't help it."

Mom says, "You know, honey, relationships change—people change and our feelings for one another change too, but this tension with Travis shouldn't be something that ruins your friendship."

"I know," I say.

Mom says, "It sounds like you've been under a ton of stress lately."

I say "Yeah," but a thought is growing inside me, something Mom and I have never talked about.

Without even knowing I'm going to say it, I just blurt out, "Why'd you stop loving Dad?"

Mom stops washing the dishes and looks at me. "I

still love your dad, and I'll always love him, just not in the ways that let us share our lives together—not like a wife needs to love her husband."

I've always been confused about how my mom and dad can be so nice to each other, such great friends, but weren't able to keep our family together.

I ask, "Why didn't you and Dad stay together, like Roy and Rita—why couldn't you do that for me, for our family?" As I hear myself ask this question, I realize it's something that's been inside me since I was seven years old, but it's a little kid's question and one that Mom just answered—she still loves Dad, just not in the ways that would let them stay married.

Mom is quiet for a few seconds. Then she says, "Your dad and I love each other as friends; we were in love once, but our ways of loving each other changed."

I remember, now, something Dad once told me back when he and Mom first split up. I was seven then, and Dad was tucking me into bed at our apartment, the first place we lived after he moved out. I asked him, "Can't you two get back together?"

"Sorry, buddy," Dad explained, "it doesn't work that way."

"Can't you make her love you?" I asked. (Hey, cut me some slack, I was only seven.)

Dad answered, "You can't make somebody love you, Scotty. Love has to be felt and then given—it's a gift, not something you can demand."

When I looked at Dad that night, I saw tears in his eyes—I knew how sad he was, how hurt he felt. Thinking back on it now, remembering how sad my dad was, I know that's the reason he and I have never talked about it since—I've never wanted to see him so sad again.

Feeling tears start to come to my eyes again, I admit to Mom the worst thing I ever felt, the scariest, hardest thing: "You know, I always thought it was something I did that made you guys break up."

She looks at me, and there're tears in her eyes too. "God no, Scotty, that's the furthest thing from the truth—why would you think that?"

I try to answer. "I don't know why, I always just

thought it. . . ." I'm unable to finish my thought. "I just don't know why, I—"

Mom interrupts, "I know why, sweetie; it's in every divorce book I ever read. A child, especially a young child, always blames him- or herself—your dad and I hoped that we handled things in a way where you wouldn't feel that; but I think that's impossible. It was *not* your fault, Scotty, you have to know that now."

"Really?" I ask, and for the first time since I was seven years old, I maybe believe it.

"Yes, *really*," Mom says.

I take a couple of deep breaths and we're quiet.

The older I get, the more complicated everything seems to be; maybe Travis is right, maybe as you grow up *baseball and bullshit* aren't enough to make life okay.

Finally I say, "Things have changed for me and Travis. I'm not sure how to be friends with him anymore, and I feel guilty."

Mom says, "Change is always scary and hard—but to love someone, you have to really know them. Travis has been afraid to be himself. Now you see the real

Travis, so you can be a real friend to him, and him to you—if you let him."

I nod and force a smile, but I think about all the stuff that's been going on with Trav. How can we get back to being friends? I wonder if he's thinking the same thing.

I watch Mom finishing the dishes, study her face as she looks out the window at the sun starting to go down. Both she and Dad have gotten older, actually almost *old*, in the time I've been alive. It's so strange, the way they've changed in how they look—Dad more than Mom, but both of them. Mom's face is like it used to be, only with more lines and wrinkles.

If my HIV test comes back saying that I have it, the news will *kill* her. My dad will be real messed up about it too, but I *know* for sure that Mom couldn't handle it. And another thing I realize now, for the first time since all this started: I know that bad news about the test would be worse for them than for me.

Okay, that's enough of that. I have to try something other than just sitting around feeling scared.

Suddenly I know exactly what I need to do. I say,

"Hey, Mom, I'm gonna go up to the studio and use the computer."

Mom asks, "School stuff?"

I lie. "Sort of."

In truth, it's not studying I want to do. I gotta Google "AIDS+HIV+third+baseman+who+gets+all+chickenbutt+for+no+reason" and see what I come up with.

Time to stop being an idiot, a self-centered, bad friend, and a wimpy wuss! Time to do some serious work on my attitude.

Final thoughts on keeping your head in the game: When I was in Little League, about ten or eleven, I decided I wanted to be a swish hitter. Not only did I not know that it was "switch," not "swish," but I had no idea about the reason why it was better to be able to hit from both sides of the plate. One day I stepped into the left-side batter's box against a hard-throwing left-handed pitcher—thank god my coach saw this, and after I struck out, he pulled me over and quietly explained the right-hand/left-hand pitcher equation in relation to switch, not swish, hitting. So here's the deal: Ignorance of something is fixable—you just have to get the right information and you're set. Stupidity, on the other hand, which often comes from being terrified and acting like a moron . . . well, that can take a bit more time to handle.

Day 4

(Friday)

Knowledge of the game: On the surface, this sounds a lot like "keeping your head in the game," but there's a difference. Knowledge of the game is based on a blend of experience and information. You keep your head in the game while you're playing it; you build your knowledge of the game before, during, and after it. Think of it this way: If you were getting ready to face a great team, you'd make a plan and build your lineup based on that plan, kind of like if you were worried that you might be infected by HIV, maybe it'd be smart to go on the internet and get some information from places like the CDC, WebMD, or MedlinePlus!

I learned a lot about AIDS and HIV last night. Stuff that helps me put my pathetic whining into perspective. Most people know that AIDS is a worldwide epidemic. But I never realized that eight thousand people die from it *every day*, eight thousand *a day*—moms, dads, even little kids. But it's also true that there are medicines now that can keep you alive for years—decades—with HIV and keep it from becoming full-fledged AIDS. Those medicines, in the United States, cost about ten thousand dollars a year, but at least they exist. More and more research is being done every day to try to lower the cost and increase the availability of these drugs. Obviously none of this is great news, but it makes a guy think, and knowing this stuff is better than thinking I'm doomed if the word is bad from my blood test. Knowing that there are ways to survive and even live with the disease makes it a little easier to calm down and to focus on other things.

Back at school this morning, everything is all right as near as I can tell. I haven't heard any mention of gay stuff. Unbelievable as it may sound, our baseball team has wiped the "secret homo" story right out of most people's minds. Yep, it's true: Baseball to the rescue. Our team is only two wins away from the high school city championship and an unprecedented undefeated season. People, a lot of them, have actually started coming out to watch us. Even the cheerleaders are coming, sitting on the front row of the bleachers. They're not allowed to stand up and cheer. It's actually kind of funny, watching them sit there as if their butts are superglued to the metal seats, waving their red and black pom-poms and trying to convert football and basketball cheers to baseball. "D-fense, D-fense, D-fense," and "Push 'em back, push 'em back, waaaayyyy back . . ."

For the last two games, the custodian and the kids on the grounds crew who help him have added a full set of additional bleachers on the third-base side, right next to the regular ones. The success of the team has helped take people's attention away from everything else.

Today after school we play the semifinal for the tournament. But right now, although I'd never say it out loud, a part of me feels like *big whoop*. This is weird, because baseball has always meant so much to me, and of all the times for me to suddenly get all easy-going about playing ball, this seems like the worst—then again, maybe it's the best.

As school rolls on, I manage to pretty much avoid Matt Tompkins. Of course, I can't avoid him completely: We *are* in three classes together, Computer Science, English, and Mr. Robinette's World History. But by arriving as late as possible for the day's classes, I haven't had to interact with him.

It's funny, though; I can't help but feel that Matt's been avoiding me, too. I haven't allowed myself any eye contact with him, so I can't be sure, but as I've passed him in the halls going to and from classes, he completely ignores me. Whatever is up with him, I don't really care, so long as he stays away from me . . . and from Trav. Yeah, I'm a hypocrite—it's okay for me to hurt my friend, but nobody else better!

As school comes to an end today, the pressure over our game this afternoon is worse than it's ever been before—it's against the team with the next-best record to ours in the league!

In the locker room as we suit up, everybody is as tight as a fish's ass. Captain Josh even tries to joke around with us, and Josh *never* clowns around. His efforts to be lightweight and relaxed make everybody even more uptight. I have dry mouth something awful.

I sit near my locker and lift my glove up to cover my mouth and nose with it. If you watch much big league baseball, you've seen the catcher call time out and go talk to the pitcher, and the pitcher often covers his mouth with his glove when he talks, as if he's scared that the batter can read lips or something. I've always suspected that the real reason pitchers hide their faces behind their gloves is the reason I'm doing it right now: I *love* the smell of my glove, the leather, the oil I rub into it a couple of times a week to keep it supersoft—it's the greatest scent in the world.

Now, lowering the glove from my face, I take a few deep breaths and try to relax. Hey, it's a baseball game, not a tsunami in Indonesia, not a hurricane on the Gulf

Coast, not an exploding troop transport in Iraq—it's just a baseball game.

Turns out we are up 9 to 2 by the third inning. Of course, with a cushy lead we are playing loose again, laughing and clowning around. It's a perfect day. The sky is ninety percent blue, with only a couple of white, fluffy clouds. We have a huge crowd. The grounds crew has added a third set of bleachers down the left-field line and a second set down right field. Whatever number of seats the ground crew sets up, every seat is taken. Even more fans, mostly kids from school, sit on the grass where the bleachers end. Dad and Travis have come to today's game. I'm not worrying about them. I'm trying to concentrate on the game itself.

By clowning a little during the game, we aren't meaning to be disrespectful to our opponents. Butler H.S. is a good team; it's just so much fun to be way ahead and not feel so much pressure.

Willie Brown, our shortstop, is a joker all the time. As he gets up to bat in the fourth inning, he gives Josh,

111

who is coaching at third base, a real goofy look, which cracks Josh up. We've been pounding the ball, especially against this kid they've brought in as a relief pitcher. He is on the mound when Willie steps up, and he sees Willie's routine. His first pitch is a fastball, hard and straight at Willie's head. The sickening *smack* of the ball exploding against Willie's batting helmet can be heard all over the field. Willie drops like he is dead.

I once saw Major League fastball pitcher Randy Johnson bean a guy. Everybody could tell Randy was real upset, and that it was an accident. Nobody came out to fight or anything, because everybody knew that it was unintentional.

The Butler pitcher, though, smiles and looks at his dugout as Willie hits the deck. He imitates Willie's goofy expression from a few seconds before. Big, *big* mistake.

The brawl is as ugly as any I've ever been involved in. Our catcher, Mark Trilling, is the first guy out of our dugout, followed by all the rest of us. Butler's guys meet us at the mound and the fists start flying. Sometimes in baseball, fights are just jokes, but an intentional beaning like this eliminates any possibility of one of those pick-a-partner, dance-around deals. Trilling aims a major right hook at the Butler pitcher's mouth. If the punch had landed squarely, the kid would still be on his knees looking for his teeth.

The fight lasts a good five minutes, which is a long time for a fight. I get lost under a pileup and spend most of my time just trying to protect myself from feet and fists coming at my face. It's scary. I finally manage to claw my way out from beneath three or four bodies and get back on my feet. I am up just in time to see Matt Tompkins do one of the nastiest, most vicious things I've ever seen.

He backs himself quickly across the infield to where the pitcher who beaned Willie is trying to hide out. Because Matt backs toward him, I'm sure the kid has no idea what's coming. When Matt is right in front of him, his back still to the kid, he cocks his arm high and swings his elbow with all his might. It connects with the pitcher's face. Matt has made it look like an accident, but I've seen his eyes as he sets it up, moving himself into position, picking the perfect moment, and then striking.

The results looks like a stunt in a movie, the way the kid's nose just explodes with blood. The kid drops, holding his face, blood flowing freely from between his fingers; he is too hurt to even moan.

When order is finally restored, the Butler pitcher doesn't have to be tossed out of the game, because he is so messed up with a broken nose that he can't return anyway. Our catcher, Mark Trilling, is thrown out. Willie, still a little shaky from the beaning, is okay; he even stays in the game.

I admit I have a temper. At my dad's, twice I've smashed the remote control for our TV, first the original and then the seventy-dollar replacement, when the Mariners lost games they should have won. I'm not proud of this—in fact, after I lose control, I always feel ashamed of myself. But after watching what Matt did today, I could tell that he was never out of control. He wasn't like I get when I go nuts. He was very methodical, very cold. At no time did Matt ever look like he was mad. To me, that makes him even scarier.

The game gets really sloppy after the brawl. We make four errors. Even Captain Josh drops a fly ball on a fairly tough try, but it's one he makes ninety-nine out of a hundred times. Matt makes two errors, on easy grounders. Still, we hold on for the win. Personally, I have a great game; I don't have any errors and I get four hits and bring home five runs.

It's a relief to contribute so big-time today. I've made only one error in the last six games. But more important than my defense, which has been good all year, today I hit again. I hit fastballs, of course, but I hit the off-speed stuff too. Actually, I hit everything! I'm in the zone. I've raised my season batting average back up to .340, with a total of eight home runs and twenty-one RBIs.

We win, but we win ugly. What a nasty baseball phrase that is, "winning ugly." To me it means that none of the good stuff about winning made any difference—not skill, not talent, not the fact that you work hard, play hard, or deserve to win, not even being lucky. Nope, winning ugly is actually more like not even winning. You have more runs on the board at the end of nine innings—but is that the reason you play? It's actually just another form of losing;

somehow, winning ugly is like my argument with Trav, because being right doesn't matter all that much. I can't explain it any better than that, but winning ugly is not a good thing.

Back in the locker room Matt sits alone, steaming. Besides his two errors, he went 0 for 4 and had two strikeouts. He can work his jaw like nobody I've ever seen, with the exception of Elvis Presley in some of those stupid *Viva Las Vegas*–type movies where he wiggles his jaw when he's acting like he's PO'd. But Elvis was pretending; as Matt works *his* jaw now, it's no act, just a big, enraged-looking carnivore that feeds on red meat and anger.

I haven't spoken to him since our World History class. And after the crappy game he played today, I have no intention of saying anything now. But as I'm finishing getting my stuff together at my locker, I feel him staring at me. I make the mistake of glancing over.

"Listen," Matt says, his voice low and cold. "I know about your little buddy. You just stay away from me."

I knew it! I start to say, "I'm not ga—"

But he interrupts. "I don't care what you are—just shut your mouth and stay away from me!"

I realize that no matter what I say, it won't help, so I shut up. Matt's always been the opposite of me. I wear my feelings pretty much right out there; with Matt, you can hardly ever tell what's going on inside him—so him saying this stuff feels dangerous for both Travis and me.

I leave the locker room and walk quickly to my truck. I unlock the door and get in. I just sit here for a while wondering: How much hotter can my hot corner get?

Knowledge of the game, final thoughts: The longer I play ball, the smarter I seem to get about it. This is not to say that I never make stupid moves, never make bad plays, and never mess up. Nope, there's no way to play without sometimes screwing up, and I think it's pretty cool that there's even a symbol for it when you're keeping score: "E" equals "error." But every error you make, if you're paying attention, you gain knowledge. I think that's called learning from your mistakes. And you don't have to play third base to experience it.

Day 5

(Saturday)

Winning and losing: In baseball there are no ties. You play until one team wins and one team loses. There's no maximum number of innings, no set number of outs, there's no time clock. So there's no other way to end a game, except by forfeit, once you've started. Every so often on a hot July day, playing a meaningless American Legion game, when you're in the top of the thirteenth and you're standing at third and there are two outs and nobody is on base— you say to yourself, Let's just call this one a draw. But you'd never say it to anyone. In baseball somebody has to win and somebody has to lose; that's the game. It's that clear-cut. Unfortunately, most other things are not quite that simple.

Saturday morning I try to phone Travis from my mom's place to talk to him about Matt, but he doesn't answer his cell. I call Dad's house too, but no one answers there either. Because it's the weekend, no school, there's nothing I can do but drive in early and try to find Trav. After what Matt said yesterday, *I know about your little buddy*, I have to give Travis a heads-up.

Normally, Coach insists that we be at the field an hour before a game, but our game today isn't like any we've ever played before—this game is the championship, so we're supposed to be in two hours before the first pitch.

I drive by Dad's house and there's no one home. I go by the Five-Mile Espresso, where Travis and Dad and I used to go for Saturday-morning donuts after Friday-night sleepovers; no luck there either.

I cruise by Roy and Rita's house, my stomach doing a small flip-flop, but neither Dad's nor Travis's car is in the driveway or parked on the street.

I glance at my watch and I'm already twenty minutes late.

I grab my cell and dial Travis's cell again. It picks up on the first ring and I leave him a voice mail. "Listen, Trav, I know this is gonna sound strange, but stay away from Matt Tompkins today, okay? I'll explain after the game."

There's nothing more I can do now except hope that Travis checks his messages and that he doesn't run into Matt anywhere this morning. There's not really any reason why Trav would see Matt, and I've done all I can do. I have to set that aside and start focusing on the game; the most important game in my life, in any of our lives.

I drive to Hart Field for our one-o'clock start time.

Parking my truck in the already packed parking lot and seeing the size of the crowd already here, over an hour and a half before the first pitch, I realize that this game, the big one, for all the marbles, is going to be something else.

Everybody in the Western world seems to be here. I don't actually know how many people are watching; maybe it'll say on the news tonight. All three local TV channels, 2, 4, and 6, have sent out their main sports guys, the ones you see reporting sports every evening at five and eleven. All I know for sure about the crowd is that it is so big that the umpires had to have the grounds crew rope off the left- and right-field foul territories all the way to the center-field fence. They also made a bunch of kids who were hanging over the fence in center field move so they weren't directly behind the pitcher. There are more people watching this game than I've ever seen at a Thompson H.S. basketball or football game, which is pretty amazing. It's packed.

I'll admit that as much as I love baseball, it can be boring sometimes if you don't know what's going on; in fact lots of times it's not very exciting. But if just once you get into a game as important as our game today is, and if it turns out to be a great one, you'll never see baseball the same way again.

•   •   •

We start out falling behind by two runs in the top of the first inning as Priest River, the other team, scores. In the bottom of the first, Josh Williams walks and then steals second. He makes it to third on a sacrifice fly to shallow right field; the play is real close with a great throw by their right fielder and an even greater head-first slide by Josh. We get a run of our own when Josh scores with two outs on my single into left.

In the second inning, nobody scores but both sides make some incredible defensive plays. Alex Turner, our right fielder, who is usually pretty weak with his glove, makes a diving catch into the crowd, where he knocks over about four fans. During the bottom half of the inning, Priest River's shortstop, a little guy, only about five foot four, makes two unbelievable plays on balls that look like sure base hits; one to his left and one to his right.

Good pitching dominates the next four innings as our pitcher, Phil Coyle, settles down and strikes out five of the next thirteen guys he faces, giving up only one harmless single. Their pitcher does an equally good job. Good pitching can be boring, but these guys are working fast—and with a score of 2–1, and our winning streak, and the league championship riding on the outcome, the crowd's really into it.

In the seventh and eighth the offenses get going again for both teams. We take our first lead of the game in the bottom of the seventh, only to have them come back and score in the top of the eighth. Going into the last inning, the game is tied 5–5. Priest River scores the go-ahead run in the top half of the ninth inning on a two-out home run by their third baseman, a tall, gangly kid with a good glove who hasn't had a base hit all day. Their team goes wild; they pour out to greet the kid who has hit the dinger and mob him. I know I should be all depressed and down, but I can't stop smiling. The winning and losing thing just doesn't matter that much. If somebody is going to beat us, I'm glad it's their guy at third base—their hot-corner man.

We get the final out in the top of the ninth and are back in our dugout. I walk up and down the line kind of laughing and chattering it up with our guys. I am doing like "Hum baby, hum baby, come on . . ." as if we're back in Little League. Several of the guys start laughing along with me, doing "Hum baby, hum baby" too. It's like we are all eleven years old again, playing rec-league ball, and nothing matters but having fun. They are up 6–5, but we have one more chance!

We have to score one run to tie—this would force the game into extra innings—or two runs to win it straight out. Of course, if we don't get at least one run, we will lose. I refuse to think about losing. I refuse to consider the possibility that our season could end in a loss. Life is full of losing and losses— ones we can't do anything about. This is only a high school baseball game, but I am not going to let us lose today—life lets us win some of the time too. I *need* to win this thing—I need this win!

I'm due up fourth. Allen Smitter, our second baseman, leads off the inning. He walks up to the plate and drives the first pitch hard up the middle for what looks like a sure base hit until that incredible little Priest River shortstop makes another absolutely fantastic play, diving from out of nowhere to snag the ball and throw

Allen out by two steps. Our coach, Mr. Trefts, pinch-hits Brad Collins for our pitcher, and Brad works a 3–2 count into a walk by fouling off two potential third strikes. Next up, batting just in front of me, is Matt Tompkins. Matt is one for three with a single in the fourth inning. He's our best power hitter, but he also leads the team in strikeouts and at hitting into double plays. If Matt can get on base or at least stay out of a double play, I'll get to hit. I'll either be the hero or the goat. My adrenaline pulses through me.

I walk to the on-deck circle and try to quiet my breathing. Inside my head I talk to myself like an ESPN Sportscenter announcer: "Collins represents the tying run and is on first. Tompkins, the big first base-man, is at bat, the potential winning run. And in the on-deck circle is Scott Latimer, two for two today with a walk, an RBI, and a run scored. It's important for Tompkins to stay out of the double play and to—"

An incredible crack of the bat interrupts my fantasy broadcast. Matt hits a one-hop dart right down the third-base line, where Priest River's third baseman, the hero of the top half of the ninth, is hugging the line.

There is no doubt that they can turn a double play to end the game—Matt hasn't even gotten out of the batter's box when the ball smacks into the third baseman's glove.

"Foul ball," the umpire calls and signals, spreading his arms out wide. Even from my spot in the on-deck circle I can see the crease in the dirt, two inches foul, five feet in front of third base.

If Matt strikes out, we'll be down to our last chance, down to my last at bat. I want it. I have played hard and practiced my whole life for this moment. A part of me is scared, but lately I've faced much bigger fears!

Matt takes a pitch, high and in for a ball, then another one low and away. Two balls and one strike. That count favors Matt, but their pitcher has pitched us well all day.

I need to clear my head, forget about failure and winning and losing, and just relax.

I look up toward the bleachers, up into the seats, hoping to catch a glimpse of my dad or mom or Travis. I need to escape from the pressure. I take a couple of slow, deep breaths and whisper, "Hum baby, hum baby," to myself, getting ready; I even smile—

Crack!

It's a sound like no other in sport: the sound of a bat crushing the life out of a hard-hit fastball. The second I hear it, I know that if it's fair, it's gone. I look up in time to see the ball sailing into the sky toward straightaway center field. Matt drops his bat, raises his arms, and starts off toward first base at a quick trot.

The ball clears the fence by a good fifty feet. Home run!

It's over.

We've won!

All of our guys, who've been pressed up against the chain-link fence of the dugout, wearing their rally caps upside down and inside out, pour onto the field, jumping up and down like maniacs. I'm stunned. Of course, I'm happy we've won! We've set a new record for consecutive wins in an undefeated season, and we are the champs. But I also feel like I've lost my last chance. As I peel off my batting gloves, I can't lock out the weirdness of Matt Tompkins being the hero. I wanted to be the hero—I needed to be! I try to put it out of my head, but it keeps rolling over and over. All my life baseball has been the most important thing, and now, at its most important moment, I'm left standing in the on-deck circle? This isn't the way I saw things going—not at all. There's a huge hole in my gut, a huge empty feeling inside me; how can this happen, to be so close to being a hero only to have it snatched away at the last second? *You live in fantasyland . . . baseball and bullshit . . . you think everything is one way, the way you wish it were, when really nothing is!*

I watch Matt trotting around second base and I realize that I'm being a jerk, a jealous jerk at that.

I remove my batting helmet and by habit drop my gloves into it. My bat lies on the ground at my feet; the metal donut ring is still wedged onto the barrel from my warm-up swings. Gloves, helmet, bat—if I don't get a call-up from the pros, this will be the last time I'll ever use this equipment. Matt is the hero, not me. How is that fair? But even as I ask myself the question, I laugh at how stupid that is—"fair" hardly ever has anything to do with what happens.

I walk out to join the rest of the team at home plate.

I crowd in next to Josh and Willie and all the other guys. It's mayhem as we all jump up and down together. The crowd pours onto the field from every direction, jumping up and down with us, waving their arms in the air, whooping and whistling and hollering. It's completely nuts. Brad Collins crosses the plate to a mugging of a hundred hugs and high-fives. By the time Matt comes around third, there is a huge mob of kids and he is actually smiling and laughing, accepting back-slaps and hugs and high-fiving kids; I don't remember *ever* seeing him laugh before.

The umpire behind home plate, getting jostled by the crowd, finally gets out of the way, giving up on the idea of watching Matt touch home. This game is over. My baseball career is probably over too. Oddly, it feels all right—actually it feels almost good.

The second Matt jumps up and lands with both feet on home plate, he is lifted onto the shoulders of dozens of crazed kids, some teammates, some classmates. They carry him off for a trip around the diamond again. I give up on the idea of trying to congratulate him—the crowd is too wild and he wouldn't care anyway. In the middle of that mob, though, I see the two girls from the Safeway. I can't remember their names—oh yeah, the taller, blond girl is Davita; I think that's right. The girls are helping carry Matt, the hero, on his victory lap. This is his moment.

I turn to leave the field, noticing for the first time all the kids surrounding me, slapping my back, excited to be close to me just because I've been a part of it. I am laughing and whooping along with everybody else. Some moments are pure *good*, and this is one of them.

I look across the white chalk running up the first-base line, and standing waiting for me are my dad and mom and Travis. Mom comes over and gives me a big hug. "I'm so proud of you," she says. Dad hugs me too and adds, "Good game, great game, you guys were magic out there."

Travis has hung back a little, but I see his face. It is obvious he doesn't want to take anything away from my moment, but I can tell he is really happy for me. How hard must it be for him to stand back and watch my parents give me so much love and support, while his parents have shut him out of their lives? Here I am being treated like a hero, when really I'm not a hero at all. Travis is the *real* hero. I get that now; he's done something brave—and it isn't in a baseball game, it's in *real* life, and it's something that matters a lot more than any game.

He steps tentatively toward me, smiling and putting his hand out for me to shake. I take his hand and use it to pull him close. I give him a big hug. It feels good, like it always used to feel when we were little and we'd wrestle with my dad, or as we got a little older and we'd be on the playground and score a winning goal or touchdown and we'd jump up and down and grab each other; it feels just right.

"Congratulations," Travis says. "You guys were awesome."

"Thanks," I say, still holding my friend close. "I'm sorry," I add softly. I feel really emotional, my throat tight and my hands kind of shaky. But it feels great to be able to apologize and mean it. "I'm so sorry," I say, "for being a jerk, for not being a better friend, for not—"

He interrupts me. "Hey, we're cool. We can talk

about all that later. Let's just enjoy this." I look into his face and he is smiling too. He's right; we're in the middle of a gigantic party, so it's definitely party time.

We both laugh and pull away from each other, and do a fairly successful high-five.

At about this moment the crowd carrying Matt on their shoulders sets him down to a huge cheer at home plate. Matt looks deliriously, out-of-his-skull happy. He waves his arms over his head to the hundreds of fans still in the stands, and they cheer wildly again.

"I better go congratulate him," Travis says, pulling away from me.

I haven't heard his words clearly, or his message just doesn't quite register in the chaos and excitement of the moment. Before I realize what's happening, Travis is walking straight toward Matt.

A rush of fear, backed by a jolt of adrenaline, blasts up my spine and into my head, exploding!

"*Travis,*" I yell to his back, lunging. He can't hear me. As I throw myself after him, I bump into a skinny girl, almost knocking her over. "Sorry," I say hurriedly, trying to pull away from her. But half a dozen other kids, jumping and screaming, are in front of me. Before I can get halfway to him, Travis is standing right in front of Matt. I see Travis's lips moving. Matt throws his head back and laughs, then he and Travis throw their arms around each other and Matt lifts Travis in the air, like a rag doll. They are both laughing and hopping up and down. I stop dead in my tracks and just watch them celebrate.

Eventually, the chaos and wildness and fun begin to ebb a little. The crowd thins out, and my mom and dad have gone.

Travis walks back up to me, smiling as he approaches.

"Jesus," I whisper to him quickly. "Didn't you get my voice mail?"

Travis says, "No, I forgot my phone at your dad's."

I say, "I thought you were going to get killed just now."

He looks puzzled, "Why?"

"Matt Tompkins"—I'm still whispering—"knows it was you in the school paper. I tried to warn you before, and again a minute ago when I couldn't get to you—"

Travis laughs and puts his hand on my shoulder. "Tryin' to rescue me, huh?" he says. "Matt's known for a couple of years, Scott."

"Years?" I ask, stunned. "Why would you tell Matt Tompkins before you told me?"

"I didn't actually 'tell' him," Travis says quietly.

I don't get it. "Well then, how'd he know?"

Travis smiles at me patiently. "That's secret, Scott. Matt's got his own reasons for needing to keep it that way."

"Matt?" I ask, suddenly grasping what Travis is saying, completely surprised. "Big, tough, rough Matt?"

"What'd you think," Travis says with a laugh, "that we all become hairdressers?"

I feel myself blush, but I smile too. "Matt," I say once more, shaking my head.

"He was pretty sure you'd react that way," Travis says. "It's the main reason he's taken such an attitude with you. But believe me, with a family like his, Matt's got to keep *real* quiet. If you think my parents have been bad, Matt's folks will *never* accept him for who he really is; they'd *hate* him. At least with my mom and dad there's still hope, I think; but not for Matty."

I smile. "Matty?" I say.

Travis blushes. "Yeah, but you probably shouldn't call him that."

Travis is telling me how important it is to protect Matt's secret. "I get it," I say. Then I add, "I've been thinking a lot about the stuff you said to me, about fantasyland, about how stupid I can be—"

Travis interrupts me. "Scott, I was out of line. I'm sorry I said that—"

I interrupt him, "No, you were right, about all of it—I have a lot of stuff to work on, but I will."

Travis says, "I was angry, but you know how much I care about you."

I say, "Yeah, I know—me too . . . but . . ." I can't think how to say it, stumbling as I try to find the right words.

But Travis laughs loudly. He says, "Believe me, Scott, you're the least gay guy I've ever met. We're friends, man—best friends, but just friends. I hope we always will be."

"Me too," I say, and I mean it.

We stand together for a while without talking, but not like it's been for this last week, not uncomfortable and bad—more like it always used to be.

"I gotta go," Travis says. "Are you staying out at the lake tonight with your mom?"

"Yeah, she's expecting me. Come on out with me— the dogs miss you."

"Nah." He laughs. "This is the last Thompson High game of the season. Your dad's gonna need somebody to help him survive toxic baseball withdrawal."

I smile and say, "You're right; thanks for filling in for me."

"Sure." Travis laughs again. "I'll see you Monday at school."

"See you," I say, and laugh.

It feels great to laugh with Travis again.

So Travis and I are still friends. If I've learned anything from all this, I guess it's two things: first, that nothing is ever quite like it seems—there's the way we imagine the world, and then there's the way the world really is;

and second, that everything in life changes, and if you fight that reality, you're gonna be miserable.

Life is not always going to be as good as this. Things don't always work out for the best. But I don't want to think about that right now. I want to feel happy for just a little bit longer. I guess that's something else I know now—being happy is more important than baseball; enjoying your life is more important than *anything*.

I'm back out at Weaver Lake. It's dark, getting late. The dogs, Evander and Bob, are asleep on the floor of the studio. I'm lying in my sleeping bag in the sleeping loft. Looking out, I see the light from the kitchen window of the house. The moon is shining down on the lake. A few crickets are chirping, and I can smell the fresh-cut grass.

In forty-eight hours I'll walk back into the Spokane Public Health office and get the results of my test. In some ways I'm not freaked out anymore. I trust Travis, and if he is infected and knows it, he'd tell me. The test should come back just fine, and besides, AIDS or no

AIDS, life is about the *way* you live, how you treat the people you love. It really is about how you play the game.

Winning and losing, final thoughts: In ways that I never really got until now, I realize that winning and losing in baseball is exactly like they always used to tell us in Little League—it doesn't matter.

Day 6
(Sunday)

Baseball history: Almost every ball player knows the history of baseball, not every bit of it, of course, but lots of the really important parts. Babe Ruth, the Black Sox Scandals, and the Red Sox finally winning the Series. Baseball history is part of the game—remembering how people have played, how they've helped make it great. History is important, I think.

A few months ago, back in early March, a month before the baseball season even began, Travis was out here for the weekend with me at Weaver Lake.

On that Saturday morning he and I walked Evander and Bob out around the lake, like we'd done on so many other Saturday mornings before. As we got to the edge of the woods and could look out and see the wheat fields ahead, Bob started a weird, low growl, and the hair on his neck rose up. Evander, who had been padding along ahead of us, stopped, then hurried back to join Bob and began to growl too. My first thought was "skunk," which is usually the nastiest thing you can run into out here. But as I looked ahead more closely, I saw what had set Bob off. It was a small herd of elk.

"Look, Trav," I whispered excitedly, although there was really no reason to whisper—they were a good 150 yards ahead and the wind was blowing toward us, so they wouldn't catch our scent. There were five of them. They were at the edge of the lake; a couple of cows were drinking, the other grazing. The bull was a big one with a huge, handsome rack, and the three cows were full-grown too. A calf stood near one of the cows, not a newborn but still small.

Travis softly said, "Wow." We leashed up the dogs and, shushing them as best we could, moved slowly toward the elk.

"We'd better not get too close," I said. The bull

looked more and more massive the closer we got. Even the cows, with a calf to protect, could be dangerous.

I'd never seen elk in the wild before. I knew they were around, but they're hard to spot. Some hunters buy elk tags every year for twenty years and never even get to fire a shot.

We walked toward them as close as we felt was safe, about fifty yards out of the woods. We were close enough to run back to the trees if they charged us. With the dogs, I knew we'd be okay so long as we weren't caught in the open.

We watched them for twenty minutes, maybe longer. When they'd had their fill of water and grazing, they walked slowly off across the field toward the bigger woods farther west.

"Pretty cool, huh, Travis?" I said.

"Yeah." He smiled.

That morning there was still even a little ice on the lake, and a small, filthy patch of snow at the foot of a craggy ledge where the sun wouldn't reach until later in the spring.

That was only a few months ago. This evening, after

hanging out with Mom, I walked Evander and Bob back out to where Travis and I had spotted the elk. Of course there were no elk to be seen, and the ice and snow are long gone. In other ways, too, it feels like there's nothing left of that morning with Travis—like the whole world has changed, all for the good. Everything that's happened these last days, everything I remember from my whole life, feels valuable and worth remembering.

It's great how sometimes, when you let yourself, you can remember the things that make you the happiest, the things that make you feel . . . I don't know what you'd call it. . . . Peaceful, I guess.

The days are getting much longer now, so even though it's close to nine P.M. by the time I get back to the studio and ready for bed, there's still a little bit of light on the western skyline.

Ten minutes ago the sun was coming through the smudged glass in streaks, oddly shaped shafts of light cutting through the pines and the leaves of the locust trees. Now the sun is low enough, and it doesn't shine directly through the windows anymore. The light is softer. At moments like this, life feels perfect—like nothing bad can ever happen.

I get my test results back tomorrow, but as worried as I've been about it, now I'm not all that nervous. Whatever the news, it'll be what it'll be and I'll deal with it.

Baseball history final thoughts: Hey, it's only baseball. What else can I say?

Day 7

(Monday)

My ride into town is quiet, just the hum of my tires over the road. I can't think of any music I want to hear. I'm still thinking a lot about everything that's happened over the last week. And, of course, I feel a little bit nervous. Who wouldn't? But in a strange way, the fear is all right.

As I park my truck and approach the building, there is one thought, one image that keeps playing over and over again in my head. Although I didn't even think about it a single time this last week, with so much going on, right now I can't stop remembering that young mother with her little boy who was here the day I got my blood drawn. She was real worried-looking, and her kid, who was totally unaware of what was happening, was wild and rambunctious, a little short-stop in the making. What's gonna happen to those two if their results come back bad? I mean, I've got my parents, Trav, my teammates, and a whole world of support in my life. What happens to the thousands of moms and little kids all over the world who have nothing like the love I get every day, if their tests come back bad?

The last time I was here and I saw that mom and her little kid, I said that seeing them creeped me out. That's not how I feel anymore. No, thinking about them now, I just feel sad and worried.

I get called into Dorothy's office. As she's telling me my results, something in her face, a kind of sadness just under her smile, makes me realize how it must be for her when she has to tell somebody the opposite news of what she's telling me right now.

I thank her for about the tenth time, and then I stand up to leave. Suddenly, without planning to do it, I reach over and hug her. She hugs me back, and it feels nice.

I walk out a locked door and down a short hallway.

When I get out the door to the outside, I run to my truck as fast as I can, almost tripping over a big bulge in the sidewalk where a tree root has pushed up and cracked the cement. I unlock my truck door, hop in, and peel out, my wheels throwing gravel up behind me as I race away. It takes me a couple of blocks to settle down and start breathing normally again.

My seven days at the hot corner are finally over. Now all I've got to do is figure out what to do with the rest of my life.

Two Months Later

Graduation was cool. Flat hats tossed in the air, hugs all around, although all I got from Matty, I mean *Matt* Tompkins was an overly firm handshake and about half a smile.

It's been a lazy summer. The most exciting thing has been Zeke Willhelm making it to the final round of the half-pipe skateboarding competition in the X-Games (he placed third, winning a bronze medal). Every evening on the five-o'clock news for the whole week, Zeke got interviewed—he looked almost normal: short hair, actually close to a shaved head but at least a natural color; you might have thought he was completely average except for the truly incredible way he rode his skateboard and the pierced gold hoop he wore in his right eyebrow. I felt proud of him; who'd have thought that Zeke Willhelm would be our graduating class's greatest jock?

I've been trying to decide what to do with my life—community college or get a job? Dad's given me the rest of July to take it easy and make my decision.

This afternoon I go out to grab the mail, something I do most days. I don't usually get much from our friendly postal delivery lady, other than junk about credit cards and my *Baseball Weekly*, which arrives most of the time on Fridays.

But when I look in the mailbox today, there is a letter for me.

I look at the return address on the envelope and I can't believe my eyes, can't believe what I'm seeing: It's from the Minnesota Twins.

I tear it open right away and read it.

I've been selected in the baseball draft.

I'm getting my shot at pro ball.

Without moving from the mailbox, I read and reread

the letter about twenty times. I'll start in triple-A ball at the Twins' club in upstate New York, the Rochester Red Wings, but first I actually get to join the big club for spring training next March in Arizona, the Cactus League!

I can hardly believe it—I reread the letter another half dozen times.

I can't wait to call Travis, who has his own apartment now, so that he can help me celebrate!

But the strangest thing is that I'm not even *happier* than I actually feel. Sure, I'm excited, and it's great news but . . . I don't know how to explain it . . . I feel happy . . . but . . .

Playing baseball takes a certain amount of guts and skill. Remembering that simple fact is enough for me after everything that happened last May.

Playing ball is a lot of fun, but I'm happy and lucky to be alive. I'm thankful for everything, not just baseball; I'm thankful for *everything* that happened during those seven days at the hot corner, and for what happens every day *away* from it too.

Acknowledgments

Special thanks, as always, are due Toni Markiet, my wonderful editor at HarperCollins Children's Books; her terrific assistants, Catherine Onder and Savina Kim; and the entire team, Phoebe Yeh et al. Thanks also to George Nicholson, Paul Rodeen, and Thaddeus Bower at Sterling Lord Literistic Inc. Thanks to various readers who helped me see the light in this story, including Stacie Wachholz and Stephanie Squicciarini. Thanks to Kelly Milner-Halls for helping with my web page and being a fellow writer, and to Crutch, Bill Egger, Ed Averett, Terry Davis, and Mikey Gurian.

Always, I am indebted to my family—my sons Jesse and Sheehan, sister Cindy, and Garren—so many Eggers that my sales are always brisk, including our favorite fellow travelers Wally and Kathy, also Bill and Nora, Peggy and Neil, Judy and Bill, Kathy and Jim

Rudolph, Aunt Kay and her wonderful kids . . . like I said, too many to name, but thanks to all of you.

I'm bound to leave out someone, so I might as well leave out a lot of you and just give this inadequate group thank-you to all not mentioned who support me. But thanks especially to the schools and libraries that continue to so vigorously defend and support my work, and to John Cole and the National Book Festival for their support as well.

Thanks finally to my readers.

—TT

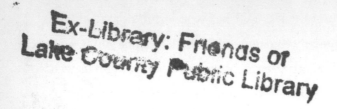